One-Handed Histories
The Eroto-Politics of Gay Male Video Pornography

T0314771

HAWORTH Gay & Lesbian Studies
John P. De Cecco, PhD
Editor in Chief

New, Recent, and Forthcoming Titles:

Gay Relationships edited by John De Cecco

Perverts by Official Order: The Campaign Against Homosexuals by the United States Navy by Lawrence R. Murphy

Bad Boys and Tough Tattoos: A Social History of the Tattoo with Gangs, Sailors, and Street-Corner Punks by Samuel M. Steward

Growing Up Gay in the South: Race, Gender, and Journeys of the Spirit by James T. Sears

Homosexuality and Sexuality: Dialogues of the Sexual Revolution, Volume I by Lawrence D. Mass

Homosexuality as Behavior and Identity: Dialogues of the Sexual Revolution, Volume II by Lawrence D. Mass

Sexuality and Eroticism Among Males in Moslem Societies edited by Arno Schmitt and Jehoeda Sofer

Understanding the Male Hustler by Samuel M. Steward

Men Who Beat the Men Who Love Them: Battered Gay Men and Domestic Violence by David Island and Patrick Letellier

The Golden Boy by James Melson

The Bisexual Option, Second Edition by Fritz Klein

Male Prostitution by Donald J. West in association with Buz de Villiers

The Second Plague of Europe: AIDS Prevention and Sexual Transmission Among Men in Western Europe by Michael Pollak

Barrack Buddies and Soldier Lovers: Dialogues with Gay Young Men in the U.S. Military by Steven Zeeland

Outing: Shattering the Conspiracy of Silence by Warren Johansson and William A. Percy

One-Handed Histories: The Eroto-Politics of Gay Male Video Pornography by John R. Burger

Sailors and Sexual Identity: Crossing the Line Between "Straight" and "Gay" in the U.S. Navy by Steven Zeeland

One-Handed Histories
The Eroto-Politics of Gay Male Video Pornography

John R. Burger

Routledge
Taylor & Francis Group

NEW YORK AND LONDON

First published 1995
The Haworth Press, Inc., 10 Alice Street, Binghamton, NY 13904-1580

This edition published 2014 by Routledge
711 Third Avenue, New York, NY 10017, USA
2 Park Square, Milton Park, Abingdon, Oxon OX14 4RN

Routledge is an imprint of the Taylor & Francis Group, an informa business

Library of Congress Cataloging-in-Publication Data

Burger, John R. (John Robert)
    One-handed histories : the eroto-politics of gay male video pornography / John R. Burger.
        p.   cm.
    Includes bibliographical references (p.   ) and index.
    ISBN 1-56024-860-2 (acid-free paper).
    1. Gay men–Sexual behavior. 2. Erotic videos. 3. Masturbation.
I. Title.
HQ76.B86 1994
306.7'086642–dc20   93-15575
                                                                                                        CIP

For Jacob, Joey, Joseph, and Denis

ABOUT THE AUTHOR

John R. Burger, MA, is Assistant Broadcast Producer with an advertising agency in New York City. An avid fan of gay male performance genres, his reviews have appeared in *Outweek* and *Newslink*. Mr. Burger received his MA in Performance Studies from New York University.

CONTENTS

Preface   ix

Chapter I. "You Must Remember This"   1

Chapter II. A Brief History of the Homoerotic Image   5

Chapter III. Visions and Revisions   21

    The Sexual Evolution   21
    Beyond Sex   33

Chapter IV. One Step Forward, Two Steps Back   53

    Backward Step #1: Racism   54
    Backward Step #2: Ageism   57
    One Step Forward: Sadomasochism   59

Chapter V. Ob/Scene   69

    The Trade   69
    Tricks of the Trade   74
    AIDS and the Trade   78

Chapter VI. Hot and Bothered: Eroto-Political Porn   85

    Sexually Active Activists   86
    A Queer Conscience   88
    Cumming and Coming Out   90

Chapter VII. Conclusion (aka–Cum Shot)   99

Appendix A   107

Appendix B   109

Appendix C   111

References   125

Suggested Reading   129

Index   135

Preface

Several years ago, while pursuing my Master of Arts degree in Performance Studies at New York University's Tisch School of the Arts, I became addictively swept up in the academic and political debates surrounding pornography and sexual representation. At the same time, new to New York, I was spending a lot of long, dateless nights at home with my VCR and the fast-forward button, consuming gay porn videos like popcorn. Consequently, my viewing habits began to inform my skills in the porn debates at school, and the results of these debates began to slant my perception of what I was jacking off over at night.

In academia I was frustrated by the dearth of scholarly information regarding gay pornography; the pornography debates were primarily constructed around heterosexual erotica, with a few token nods toward the homosexual pocket of the genre. There were, of course, short articles and book chapters focusing on gay pornography, but most only told me about narrative structure, or that gay porn is good because it shows gay sexual activity, or that gay porn is bad because it offends Andrea Dworkin. Nobody could tell me why I was so physically and intellectually attracted to it. Something far greater than erotic titillation was happening to me when I watched these videos.

I then began to move away from the majority of academic texts regarding the subject (having consumed or rejected a good number of them), turning instead to the many different manifestations of gay pornography to gather my information: videos, magazines, and odd industry ephemera. Porn star interviews on *The Robin Byrd Show* and video consumer catalogues became my preferred texts. Although anthropologically uninformed, I pursued my studies, nonetheless, like a cultural anthropologist. In fact, it was in an anthropology class that I first discovered the work of the Popular Memory Group and its notion of popular memory, which so greatly influences this book. It seemed to me that the people who were *talking* about gay pornography (I highly doubt if they were watching much of it) were missing or ignoring a lot of what was contained therein. Gay pornography seemed to me to be a warehouse of our cultural heritage and memory, as well as an important site for the production and modification of this heritage and memory.

Thus I began. Friends laughed because, for me, voyeurism and masturbation became scholarly processes. Video viewing became both an erotic and academic mania. Not only did I just want to keep seeing more and better sex, I also had to keep up with the changing trends in the industry for the purposes of this study. In fact, I still occasionally suffer from academic anxiety over this book, knowing full well that in the period between its completion and its publication, certain important changes are likely to occur in the genre.

Be that as it may, I continue to avidly view gay porn videos. Even though, three years later, nights are not so dateless anymore, I still get a cerebral erection from these one-handed histories.

This book would not have been possible without the mental, physical, and emotional support of my friends and family. I would like especially to thank my extended family, to whom this book is dedicated, and my parents, for their continued love throughout my life. I am also indebted to the friends who were there to help me through those late-night anxiety attacks and informational lapses, and whose encouragement and excitement gave me that extra boost of energy when needed: Terrence Carey, Michael Freiberg, Tamara Friedman, Julie Hunt, Mark Jones, Buzzy Renard, Alison Sloane, Chris Whipp, and David Young, and Vince Migliore and the staff of Gay Pleasures. Finally, I am grateful for the guidance given and intellectual challenge posed by Peggy Phelan, Richard Schechner, Allen Feldman, Brooks McNamara, and the rest of the faculty of the Performance Studies Department at New York University, who bestowed upon the first incarnation of this book the Leigh George Odom Memorial Prize for Distinguished Masters Thesis.

Chapter I

"You Must Remember This"

It is not much of a secret to gay men that, diverse as we are, we *are* everywhere. Homosexuals serve in the military, participate in organized sports, work at construction sites, occupy positions in church, state, schools, and law offices, and have graced the annals of history, from Caesar's Rome to the expansion of America's Wild West, through World War II, and on. It is also not much of a secret to gay men that our presence in such settings goes unacknowledged by most everyone else–and that many do more than ignore this presence, they work to conceal it. For numerous reasons, the voices of the gay communities (and here I speak primarily of the Euro-American gay communities) have been continually silenced throughout history. The hegemonic social structure of the United States is predicated upon the power wielded by middle- to upper-middle-class white heterosexual Christian males. Historically, groups or individuals that did not fit snugly into this category were systematically marginalized, rendered voiceless, invisible, and powerless–and to varying degrees, they remain so. The many recent gains made by the gay communities do not erase the continuing attempts by this society to retain its control over various minorities.

There are many social constructs which are used and manipulated by this hegemony to maintain its power and silencing influence over these marginal communities. Concepts of gender, sexuality, the public/private dichotomy, and average community standards are imbued with mythic essentialist traits, supposedly reflecting the norms of the American public as a whole. For example, sexuality is, supposedly, about procreation. This in turn implies a male/female coupling, as well as the privileging of biological processes over carnal pleasures. Therefore, gay men (and lesbians) are, given the status quo, constructed as deviant pleasure-seekers who have rejected both their divinely and biologically predetermined purposes. The practice of sex with the sole aim of erotic gratification is sinful, such practitioners are sinners, and their punishment is marginalization here, damnation in the hereafter.

Fear of the "other" (that is, those who celebrate a certain emancipation from the absolutist strictures of religion and science) compels this society, governed by God-fearing and biologically dutiful heterosexuals, to react in racist, sexist, homophobic ways. Aside from the frighteningly common incidents of fag-bashing, rape, and racial bias, one manifestation of this fear, of which all marginal communities in the United States are objects, is the disallowance of their historicization. Without access to the dominant modes of historicization (text books, media, national monuments, and museums, to name but a few), these marginal groups are rendered invisible, excluded from history.

But "invisibility" and "history" are relative terms. What the dominant social order promotes as history is, of course, not the whole story. The histories of marginal communities may be unknown to those folks content to swallow the White Man's offerings, but they are by no means unknown to members of those communities. What is at work here is a power-play centered around semantics. "History" generally means *official* history, visibly embodied. That is, if it is written in a text book or memorialized in a national monument, it must be true. Those events, those states of being which are not publicly concretized by the social order are not "history."

What certainly exists, at least within the marginal communities themselves, is *popular memory*. The term *popular memory* denotes the social production of memory, the different ways in which a sense of both the past and present is constructed by and within a culture's smaller communities. It is directly opposed to, but not altogether immune to the influences of, dominant memory. Dominant memory is the production of memory by the governing social order. The Popular Memory Group, a British cultural studies collective, has set forth in its manifesto "Popular Memory: Theory, Politics, Method," valuable hypotheses regarding the construction of popular memory. A number of these hypotheses help form the basis for this study of gay male video pornography.

In order to get the whole picture, to obtain an inclusive reading of the complexities of American history, it is necessary, in the words of the Popular Memory Group, to

> include all the ways in which a sense of the past is constructed in our society. These do not necessarily take a written or literary form. Still less do they conform to academic standards of scholarship or canons of truthfulness. Academic history has a particular place in a much larger process. We will call this "the social production of memory." In this collective production everyone participates, though unequally. Everyone, in this sense, is a historian. (1982, p. 207)

In constructing its past, the marginalized community is, in a sense, rewriting "history." In this sense, popular memory is also a "dimension of political practice" as well as an "object of study" (Ibid., p. 205). It is important to note here that memory does not exclusively refer to the past. Memory is about the "past-present relation. It is because 'the past' has this living active existence in the present that it matters so much politically" (Ibid., p. 211). So in looking at a community's construction of the past, one is also looking at its construction of the present and, consequently, its construction of potential futurity (i.e., becoming a recognized and participating factor of the dominant memory).

What are some of the ways, then, in which gay men in America construct a sense of their past? Such means include autobiographies, personal letters, quilting, guerrilla art, specialized and narrowly distributed academic texts, public access cable television, and pornography. Although each of these means is an important purveyor of gay male histories and truths, pornography (specifically video pornography) is a most underestimated and misunderstood manifestation of gay popular memory.

The production and proliferation of gay male porn, gaining its momentum from the 1969 Stonewall riots, is just one of the many paths the gay liberation movement took. If, in the early 1970s, the production, owning, and viewing of pornography was a "right" of straight men, it was now also a "right" of gay men. More importantly, however, the appropriation by gay men of pornographic media was a big step toward legitimating and making visible their sexual practices. Most social movements appropriate and recodify the languages of the existing dominant social order they wish to change. Therefore, if gay men were (and still are) constructed on the basis of sex and sexuality, they must necessarily take those constructions by and for the "other," and remake them on their own terms.

Gay male film and video pornography fulfills this premise. Under the aegis of popular memory, it works in a twofold manner: first, as an object of study, it can be read by both gays and nongays alike, as a cultural document. Second, as a dimension of political practice, it abets the reshaping, reformulation, and rethinking of gay male culture and its role in society. In short, pornography makes gay men visible. It is important to note here that in discussing gay male porn as an example of gay male popular memory, I speak of its cultural implications. I suggest that although this genre of pornography is indeed about gay male sex and desire and the hidden history of homosexuality, it is also about much more than that. I intend to look at gay male porn as an attempt by gays to rewrite themselves into American history. This is, of course, only one of many possible interpretations of the form, content, and efficacy of gay male sex films.

Chapter II

A Brief History of the Homoerotic Image

The scope of this book is intentionally limited, including only commercial gay male film and video pornography, excluding magazines, still photography, audio tapes, phone sex, artwork, and any other porn outlets. This is done for one reason: video pornography, because of its "live" and explicit nature, represents male homosexual sex more fully than the other formats. Film and video document the kinesthetics of man-to-man sex: the motions, the pacing, the pick-up, the cruise, the dialogue, the occasions of emotional interaction, the sounds. In terms of the fantasy of porn, film and video allow for the addition of musical scores and fictional narratives; editing technology permits the extension or condensation of the sexual event: premature ejaculation or difficulty achieving erection or orgasm are no longer problems. Film and video porn, then, document the state of sexual existence gay men enjoy; at the same time, they present idealized fantasy images of this existence. Gay male pornography serves both as cultural document and erotic tool. To more clearly understand gay pornography in its current manifestation, it is helpful to briefly note the extensive history of homoerotic images and gay sexual representation in the arts and media.

* * *

Male homosexual pornography has apparently existed as long as heterosexual pornography. Among early extant examples are numerous artifacts (pottery, murals, statuary) depicting male homosexual acts dating from early fifth century B.C. Greece to the reign of Pompeii (destroyed A.D. 79). However, many explicit homosexual images dating up until the late eighteenth century have been destroyed by oppressive religious leaders and censoring governments. Fortunately, many less explicit homoerotic images have survived history's censorship: Michelangelo's David, a bevy of naked Christians ranging from Medieval Christs to Renaissance St. Sebastians, and pond-fuls of post-Impressionist skinnydipping boys.

The most explicit representations of the homosexual, or merely homoerotic, male appear with the invention of photography in 1839 by Louis Daguerre. The development of the photographic representations of the nude male begin mostly as academic, medical, and anthropological studies. By 1870, however, the male physique begins to enjoy an aestheticization: both the photograph and the physique are considered "artistic." One of the first male pinup sensations was circus strongman Eugen Sandow, whose modeling career was at its peak in 1893. Regarding the purposes of physique photography, David Chapman explains:

> A physique photograph's first purpose is quite simple: to display physical development. If it does not fulfill this goal, the picture simply does not fit into the category of a physique photograph. The second purpose is to display that development in a beautiful, striking, original, and artistic way. If the photographer has done his work well, then the final result ought to portray the body faithfully and be aesthetically pleasing. (1989, p. 6)

To this I add a third purpose: to induce masturbatory fantasies in the viewer. Many of the physique models posed in the nude. Such photos were subsequently "cleaned up" by the censors. Fig leaves or simple black shadows were drawn over the nude models' genitals in pen and ink so as not to appeal to those with less than aesthetic interests. Those prurient enough, however, soon discovered that such fig leaves were easily washed or scraped away from the photographs, thus revealing what was previously only imaginable. Unfortunately, the above censorious practice also ruined many of the photographs produced at the time, and very few untouched examples exist today.

European photographers of the same era fared much better than their American counterparts when it came to representing the nude male. Vincenzo Galdi and Baron Wilhelm von Gloeden, both working at the turn of the century, exquisitely captured the nude male form in sepia prints. Baron von Gloeden primarily photographed Sicilian and North African youths, often coupling them in languid and homoerotic poses.

As for the naked male body in motion, it can be said that Eadweard Muybridge laid the groundwork for film pornography, both straight and gay (Williams 1989), with the beginning of his sequential action image studies in 1872. The first examples of motion-picture hardcore sex, however, are traceable to the advent of the stag film in the early 1900s. According to historian Tom Waugh:

> The "stag film" may be defined historically as an explicit sexual narrative, produced and distributed, usually commercially, to clandestine, nontheatrical male audiences between 1908 and 1970, principally in Europe and the Americas. (1992, p. 6)

Explicit male-to-male sexual scenarios crept into these early stag films. One of the earliest films with such a scene is the French *Le Menage Moderne Du Madame Butterfly* (c.1920). Other films of the same period with similar content, duly catalogued by Waugh, include: *La Maitresse Du Capitaine De Meydeux* (*The Exclusive Sailor*, 1924), *Le Telegraphiste* (1921-26), *Surprise of a Knight* (c.1930), *Piccolo Pete* (c.1935), and *A Stiff Game* (1930s). The sexual content and meaning of these films are very straightforward. As Waugh explains: "[A]ll present homosexual behavior in the context of heterosexual hegemony" (Ibid.). It is understood that the men in these films who are passively homosexual (i.e., they suck and get fucked) are being punished or victimized–in essence, effeminized–by a stronger, more masculine and dominating heterosexual superior. *The Surprise of a Knight* is the exception to this rule, although it is constructed around a *faux* heterosexuality; that is, one of the sexual participants is a man in female drag. This drag is not dropped until after the sex has been consummated and the poseur has revealed his penis to the viewing audience. What the other man thinks of this and whether, in the fictional context of the film, he is aware of his partner's gender is unknown.

The next milestone in the history of the filmic representation of the homoerotic comes in 1945 with Bob Mizer and the founding of the Athletic Model Guild (AMG). Mizer diligently set about creating some of the most artful and erotic male physique photography of the twentieth century, all with a decidedly homoerotic bent. In the 1950s, Mizer went on to make films for AMG, but never gave up the still photography, which he sold in individual photo sets and published in his magazine *Physique Pictorial* (founded in 1951). In fact, shortly after the first publication of *Physique Pictorial* vice officers raided the AMG studio, and Mizer subsequently lost the ensuing lawsuit against him. Eventually, the case was overturned in his favor by an appellate court which declared "the male rump is not necessarily obscene," (quoted in Siebenand 1975, pp. 44-5).

Mizer's films are rife with homoerotic imagery and fetishism, focusing in particular on leatherboy street toughs, often getting their comeuppance at the spanking hands of an overpowering, half-naked bodybuilder. Another popular theme of the AMG films is the Hollywood epic. *Ben Hur*, *Cleopatra*, and *The Ten Commandments* find their homoerotic apotheosis in AMG reels like *Aztec Sacrifice*, *Boy Slaves for Sale*, and *The Slave Fights Back*. In the 1960s obscenity laws became less strict and Mizer made the transition to nude photography. In the 1960s obscenity laws became less strict and Mizer made the transition to nude photography and, following a lenient 1968 Supreme Court ruling on obscenity, nude films–termed "backyard cock danglers" at the time (Ibid, p. 17). The Hollywood epic fad passed, but the street tough, fraternity hazing, and military school discipline scenarios all remained intact. AMG saw the end of its heyday in the early 1970s, when hardcore pornography flooded the market. Mizer had no interest in pursuing hardcore, and faded into relative anonymity, continuing to produce films and photos until his death on May 12, 1992.

Mizer had three equally popular contemporaries who also began their careers in the late 1940s, only one of whom contributed to the physique film repertoire. Bruce Bellas, a one-time staff photographer for Joe Weider, founded his Bruce of Los Angeles studio in the late 1940s. His physique photos are in the same league with Mizer's, but they do not demonstrate the same control over the artistic juxtaposing of homoerotic fetishism with the camp appeal of Hollywood. The same can be said of photographer Don Whitman who, in 1947, founded the Western Photography Guild. Whitman's studio excelled in the great outdoors as showcase for the male physique: the posing strap meets Ansel Adams. And Richard Fontaine was responsible for a number of physique films with themes similar to those of the AMG films. A notable exception is *The Days of Greek Gods* in which Fontaine (a physique star himself) and several other bodybuilders strike popular poses and then dissolve into costumed embodiments of Greek gods and ancient heroes, as a voice-over narrative explains the physiological similarities between model and myth. Although Bruce, Whitman, and Fontaine all adapted easily to the lessening moral strictures of the 1960s and incorporated nudity and more blatant homoeroticism into their bodies of work, none of them made the subsequent transition to hardcore gay pornography.

The period following World War II was a fertile one in the production of homoerotic images. Not only were the above physique photographers coming into their own, but many experimental and underground filmmakers began pushing the limits of acceptable homoerotic content. In 1947, Kenneth Anger released *Fireworks*, his first film. The movie is a paean to phallic symbols, men's rooms, sailors, cruising and its potential dangers. Three years later, Jean Genet directed his only film, *Un Chant D'Amour*. In this film Genet exposes an overtly homosexual world with explicit images of jail-house sex, replete with erections, masturbation, and romantic homo dream-romps through the forest. Genet's images are not only gay-positive, they are sex-positive as well. *Un Chant D'Amour*, possibly influenced by *Fireworks*, was, in turn, very influential on the direction later underground filmmakers were to take in their own projects of a homoerotic nature. Such films include Jack Smith's *Flaming Creatures* (1963), with its drag queens and flaccid penises, Kenneth Anger's *Scorpio Rising*, a celebration of leatherboy fetishism (also including brief glimpses of flaccid penises), and the early films of Andy Warhol: *Couch* (1964), *My Hustler* (1965), and *Lonesome Cowboys* (1967), among others.

In separate incidents in 1964, on both North American coasts, *Un Chant D'Amour*, *Flaming Creatures*, and *Scorpio Rising* were all confiscated and brought to trial on obscenity charges (an earlier precedent for such actions against homoerotic film is the 1958 lawsuit against the Coronet Theater in Los Angeles for screening Anger's *Fireworks*). The trials won widespread public notoriety. The case against *Un Chant D'Amour* was dismissed in New York, whereas on the West Coast the film was banned in Berkeley. Also in

New York, *Flaming Creatures* was declared obscene. Such notoriety only increased the subsequent bumper crop of homoerotic underground films, as best exemplified by the early Warhol *oeuvre*.

This 20-year period of homoerotic underground filmmaking documents an interesting psychological transition in the gay male communities. Richard Dyer succinctly states:

> The gay underground films of the sixties were very different from those of the late forties. The earlier films were carefully made studies of an inner gay consciousness that was taken to be the filmmaker's own; the later films were apparently artless depictions of the exterior forms of gay life. The troubled young men in *Fireworks* and *Twice a Man* [1962-3, Gregory Markopoulos] give way to the incandescent drag queens and sullen hustlers of *Flaming Creatures* and *Couch*. This change has to do with both the social perception of homosexuals and with the convergence of new ideas in the arts and the gay sub-culture. (1990, p. 134)

By the time Warhol hits the scene with his films, the "artless depictions of the exterior forms of gay life" become so exterior as to not even incorporate a documenting auteur: Warhol is reputed to have, quite often, started the camera rolling and walked out of the room, letting the machine itself capture the incipient homo-action. Warhol's sense of homosexuality (both his own and in general), although incorporating homoeroticism and camp (like the films of his contemporaries), was really about distance: being at a distance (because of his homosexuality and fame) from society at large, and, to a degree, being at a distance from his work. Mark Finch, in his essay on *Lonesome Cowboys*, attempts to explicate Warhol's tricky take on the subject. Did the artist intend the film to be a political statement? Pornography? Failed Pornography? "The sense is not of Warhol trying by failing, but of someone who can't even be bothered to pretend. It's not that the film is failed porn; it just doesn't want to bother" (Finch 1989, p. 115). This artistic apex of homo-malaise was short-lived, for in 1967 when *Lonesome Cowboys* was released, the historic Stonewall riots were only two years away. Warhol himself even went on hiatus from his homoerotic films after *Lonesome Cowboys*. In 1968 he made *Blue Movie* (aka *Fuck*), focusing on a heterosexual coupling, and then passed on the directorial banner to Paul Morrissey, who released *Flesh* that same year. *Flesh* is an ersatz underground gay film, sometimes homoerotic when focusing on always-naked, ever-flaccid hustler Joe Dallesandro interacting with his male johns, drag queen companions, and lesbian wife, but more often than not the narrative extols Dallesandro's search for heterosexual niceties.

It is interesting to look at the span of Dallesandro's early career, for it encompasses many different aspects of the evolution of the homoerotic film, and provides a gauge by which to measure the success of the movement.

Among Dallesandro's first experiences in the genre were his modeling sessions for physique photographers Bob Mizer and Bruce of Los Angeles. The dates of the sessions are inexact. Art collector Volker Janssen dates the Bruce of Los Angeles sessions circa 1960. Dallesandro appears unchanged in the Mizer photos, dated in Leyland (1982) merely to the 1960s; the model's statistics state he was 19 years of age at the time of the Mizer shoot.

In 1967, Dallesandro worked on two films with Andy Warhol: *The Loves of Ondine* and *Lonesome Cowboys*. In both films, Dallesandro participates in very blatant homoerotic activity; allowing Ondine to nuzzle his crotch in the former film, and campily alluding to an incipient elopement with Tom Hompertz in the latter. Via his physique modeling and Warhol work, Dallesandro began to achieve a well-established position as a gay cult idol.

His next movie, *Flesh*, (1968), was directed by Paul Morrissey and produced by Andy Warhol. Dallesandro becomes less homo-oriented in this film. He prefers women, and has actually fathered a child for which he deeply cares, but will still turn male tricks in order to pay the rent. Dallesandro did not appear in another Warhol/ Morrissey film until 1970. In fact, neither Warhol or Morrissey produced a Factory film between 1968 and 1970. By this time, the Stonewall riots had occurred and gay pride and visibility were quickly becoming more predominant. Homoerotic content in underground films was, in the public eye, much less daring, and sexual ambiguity no longer de rigueur. Consequently, Dallesandro consistently becomes less gay in his films over the next few years. *Trash*, made in 1970, merely implies that Dallesandro has tentative connections with the gay subculture through his interaction with drag queen Holly Woodlawn. By 1972, Dallesandro is completely heterosexual in the film *Heat*, jumping in and out of bed with Pat Ast, Sylvia Miles, and others, and never once appearing fully nude. In fact, he has undergone an almost complete de-eroticization. Dallesandro's heyday as a sexual icon is waning by 1974, when both *Andy Warhol's Frankenstein* and *Andy Warhol's Dracula* were produced. The films prior to 1974 all focus on Dallesandro's polysexuality. His sex life gives the films their narrative impetus. *Frankenstein* and *Dracula*, however, display Dallesandro as a monster-movie superhero who has sex with women (although in *Dracula*, by deflowering virgins, he saves them from the vampire's bite), and lolls around in states of undress. But he no longer embodies the homoerotic sexual prowess of his pre-1968 career. As gay men came charging out of the closets, Dallesandro and his queer film persona surreptitiously crept back in.

Concomitant with the dissolution of Dallesandro's (homo)erotic persona is the dissolution of his American film career. In 1975 he went to Europe and appeared in a string of obscure movies, most of which were never released in the United States. Although he has since been cast in minor roles in several domestic films, most notably Francis Ford Coppola's *The Cotton Club* (1985), John Waters' *Cry Baby* (1990), and Tamra Davis' *GunCrazy* (1992), Dallesandro has not enjoyed the same level of cult status he achieved in the 1960s as a primarily gay, and secondarily sexual, movie icon.

An interesting tangential note regarding Dallesandro's work in homoerotic film regards the 1977 gay porn feature *Hot House* (Hand in Hand)[*], directed by Jack Deveau. Included within the movie is a segment in which several of the characters screen a black and white eight-millimeter gay porn loop. The loop features two men, one of whom appears to be Dallesandro (in, for him, a nontraditional passive role). John Rowberry, compiler of *The Adam*

---

[*] This, and all subsequent company names parenthetically following a porn title, refer only to the current video distributor. For the most part, the dates in parentheses refer to the original film release date. In other cases, especially where the film has been later transferred to video, it is the video release date.

*Film World 1992 Directory: Gay Adult Video,** states that the actor in the film-within-a-film is definitely Little Joe (1991, p. 162). In an update to that same publication, Rowberry amends his statement: "While Jack is helping the upstairs neighbor climb in a window, some of his visitors enjoy a black and white hardcore film (in which Joe Dallesandro allegedly appears)" (1992, p. 20). And by 1993, Rowberry states: "The short film of Dellesandro [*sic*] has always been a hotly-contested item, but the tattoo on his arm is a dead giveaway," (1993, p. 90). The eight-millimeter film is of very poor quality, especially after having been filmed again. The actor most definitely appears to be Dallesandro. The haircut is similar to that which he sported in 1967 during *Lonesome Cowboys* (in between his biker-boy greased-hair phase of the early 1960s, and his Native American look of 1970). The actor in the film indeed has a tattoo of a shape similar to Dallesandro's, and it is on the same arm. Due to the poor quality of the filmed film, however, one cannot clearly discern the telltale "Little Joe" insignia. But the impish smile he beams as he gets fucked by his partner is unmistakable.

An educated guess puts the date of this underground hardcore stag film at 1965. If this is indeed the case, and if the performer is Joe Dallesandro, it positions Dallesandro as a vital and key player in the late twentieth century evolution of homoerotica and gay hardcore pornography. Beginning with his physique posing sessions, continuing through his illicit stag film appearance and his homo-experimental ventures with Warhol and Morrissey, his career comes full circle in 1977 when Deveau incorporates Little Joe's once illegal hardcore queer performance into the then seven-year-old practice of producing legalized gay male pornography. Dallesandro, in a sense, has been through it all. He is an inadvertent embodiment of the post-1960 development of gay male sexual representation. It is interesting to note that the end of his heyday coincides with his progressive rejection of his sexuality (whether homo-, bi-, or hetero-). This is not to

---

*This yearly publication (with occasional smaller updates) is a glossary magazine/handbook, replete with film stills, for the gay video consumer. It gives video plot synopses, erotic ratings and reviews, minor historical information, actor and director biographies and filmographies, and theme categorization. Although essentially a pornographic magazine itself, this publication is a valuable asset to the scholar of gay pornography and, as such, is referred to often in this study.

suggest that the one led to the other. Little Joe, however, still lives on as a gay sex icon through his AMG photos and his early films–a telling signal that the public market for homoerotic images was, and continues to be, very strong, and that breaking out of one's pop culture stereotype is incredibly difficult and not often lucrative. And recently, Dallesandro has attempted to reclaim his place in the pantheon of polysexual icons, by asserting his bisexuality in an *Advocate* interview: "I wouldn't have problems going to bed with a man or a woman . . . . In the 60's when people used to ask me 'What's your sexual persuasion?' I'd say 'Well, I wouldn't throw Mick Jagger out of bed . . . But today I would. Just because now he's so fucking ugly" (Brantley 1993, p. 79).

During the late 1960s pornography was steadily moving above ground, becoming more hard-core, and rapidly expanding as a "big business." In terms of gay-male-specific hard-core commercial pornography, the period between June 27, 1969 and September 30, 1970 is instrumental in the commercial inception and subsequent profitability of the genre. Prior to this period, particularly in 1968, the Park Theater in Los Angeles began screening soft-core homoerotic films by Bob Mizer, Pat Rocco, and others, often billed along with earlier homoerotic works of Anger and Cocteau, and sometimes with "gay interest" films such as *Some Like It Hot*.

On June 27, 1969, angry New York City drag queens began the Stonewall riots, essentially advocating gay rights and queer visibility. This date is widely recognized as the starting point of the modern gay liberation movement. Little more than a year later, President Richard Nixon received the *Report* of the Commission on Pornography and Obscenity (originally authorized by the United States Senate in October, 1967, and appointed by President Lyndon Johnson in January of 1968). The *Report* states that "[t]he Commission recommends that federal, state, and local legislation prohibiting the sale, exhibition, or distribution of sexual materials to consenting adults be repealed" (quoted in Kendrick 1987, p. 216). Although rejected by both the United States Senate and President Nixon, the Commission's *Report* essentially opened the floodgates for the already growing hard-core porn industry. The relative contemporaneousness of this event and Stonewall allowed for the widespread production and dissemination of gay male pornography.

According to Rowberry (1991), the first commercial hardcore gay porn films were released in 1970. His catalogue includes *Cycle Studs* (Le Salon), *The Diary* (Bijou), *Honorable Jones* (PM Productions), and *Long John* (PM Productions). Months are not listed, so it is difficult to know whether these films were pre- or post-*Report*. These films are unspectacular both in terms of their erotic content and their aesthetic presentation. They merely hold historic interest as being among the first commercial gay male hardcore films released. It is likely that many other films were produced at this time but have, unfortunately, been lost, due mostly to the progress of media technology. Many smaller porn production companies were unable to meet the consumer demand for home video, which surfaced in the early 1980s (the June 1982 issue of *Drummer* contains an article entitled "The Video Explosion" which hails the advent of this new visual home technology). Film-to-videotape transfer and the subsequent packaging, marketing, and distribution of videos is a costly procedure. Unable to compete in this new marketplace, many companies went out of business, and many of their eight- and 16-millimeter film loops were lost.

The early gay porn films of 1970 and 1971 were not very successful, monetarily or aesthetically. Gay filmmakers were still searching for a distinct filmic language with which to present their newly gained freedom of sexual expression. By 1972, however, a small group of directors began to explore the boundaries of pornographic movie making, incorporating the predominant representational ideologies of underground and, to a lesser degree, mainstream film. The earlier works of Anger, Genet, Smith, Markopoulos, and Warhol were invoked to aesthetically substantiate this new wave of gay fuck flicks.

One of the earliest examples of gay porn paying homage to, and mimicking, its underground predecessors is *Pink Narcissus* (1971, Sunsex Video). Essentially soft-core, the film, with its rambling camp episodes, is a technicolor amalgam of *Flaming Creatures*, *Inauguration of the Pleasuredome*, and the homo-fetishism of the early AMG loops (see also Dyer 1990). It is not surprising to find among its dramatis personae actor Charles Ludlam (in a nonpornographic role) who, in 1967, founded New York City's Ridiculous Theatrical Company. Ludlam's participation exemplifies the film's overall camp temperament. A subtler camp signifier not to be overlooked is the lead actor's stage name, Bobby Kendall. When dissected, this nominative pun breaks down to Barbie/Ken Doll–a perfect indicator of the plasticness (manifested literally in the gaudy fake butterfly which bookends the film) in which *Pink Narcissus* joyfully wallows. Perhaps *New York Times* film critic Vincent Canby best captures the film's elusive quality: "*Pink Narcissus* is a fragile antique, a passive, tackily decorated surreal fantasy out of that pre-gay activist era when homosexuals hid out in closets and read novels about sensitive young men who committed suicide because they could not go on . . . It is sad and very vulnerable and as serious as it is sappy . . ." (quoted in Turan and Zito 1974, p. 191).

On December 29, 1971, Wakefield Poole's *Boys in the Sand*, starring soon-to-be gay porn superstar Casey Donovan, opened at the Fifty-fifth Street Playhouse in Manhattan. The technical proficiency of the director and crew make the film resemble a low-budget, mainstream Hollywood release, whereas its disjointed narrative and pornographic content more readily echo the avant-gardists. *Boys in the Sand* "was advertised in mainstream newspapers, was reviewed by *Variety*, and, at $24,655, made its Top Fifty gross list for the week (the film initially cost about $20,000 to produce, market, and release). The film ran for 19 weeks in its initial engagement, and for nine weeks at the Paris Theatre in Los Angeles" (Douglas 1992, p. 69). By the summer of 1972, the film had grossed $140,000 (Poole 1972, p. 22). The positive and widespread public reception of *Boys in the Sand* marks an important turning point in the history of gay porn film production. Director Poole pointed the way to a mostly untapped profitable market: gay men starved for positive, out-of-the-closet movie representations of their selves and their (explicit) sexuality, and "almost single-handedly legitimized the gay hard-core Film" (Turan and Zito 1974, p. 197).

Nineteen seventy-two was a landmark year which also saw the release of three other important gay porn films: *L.A. Plays Itself*, released in conjunction with the film short *Sex Garage* (both HIS Video), and *Sextool* (Cosco), all directed by Fred Halsted, and *Born to Raise Hell* (Marathon), directed by Roger Earl. Whereas the earlier *Boys in the Sand* presents an idyllic view of gay sexuality, the above films all focus primarily on gay male sadomasochistic practices, mostly devoid of any traces of tenderness or romance. Although these movies echo the experimental filmmaking techniques of the 1960s underground, it is in the graphic presentation of this sexual subculture that the experimentation lies.

Richard Dyer has written substantially on Halsted's work, particularly *L.A. Plays Itself* and *Sex Garage*. Linking these two porn films with their underground heritage, Dyer states:

> Here s/m, bondage and fistfucking are intercut with a welter of images from popular culture to the accompaniment of rock music, more hectically than *Scorpio Rising* but very much evoking the feeling of that film, which is more explicitly evoked in director Fred Halsted's next film, *Sex Garage*. Both films suggest aspects of where gay porn would mainly go, towards conventional film style and macho sexuality, while also retaining the visionary, playful and self-reflexive qualities of underground cinema. (1990, p. 172)

Sextool, Halsted's next film, is often considered his masterpiece. Again there is the evocation of the early avant-gardists. The film opens on a party hosted by a drag queen, where all the principal performers congregate before embarking on their sexual journeys. The audible party chatter, however, accompanies them on their separate experiences, mixed in with an "unearthly soundtrack" (Rowberry 1986, p. 106), which invokes a surrealistic experience while viewing the out-of-the-ordinary sex acts. Fistfucking, genitorture, and the like are elevated to an almost hallucinogenic and visionary plateau in this film.

However, the pinnacle of all gay s/m pornography, both past and present, is *Born to Raise Hell*. The film is much less reliant on the tropes of the gay underground cinema than Halsted's films; there are few experimental editorial, cinematographic, or audio techniques, except for the inclusion of a dream sequence (a narrative structure very indicative of experimental film). Still, director Earl managed to make one of the most underground-looking porn features ever. The surf music soundtrack, laid back against incessant images of water sports, is a campy, underground filmic pun. The film has a grungy, down-and-dirty look, which is only heightened by the extreme explicitness of its sexual content. In fact, Earl's experimentation was not so much with the medium as with the message. Water sports, fistfucking, bondage, and severe discipline are all performed with a manic intensity which accosts the audience unlike any other gay film (pornographic, underground, or whatever) up until that time. Whereas Halstead's depictions of s/m are "arty" and often obscured, Earl's are intensely straightforward. Today, *Born to Raise Hell* is still shocking and confrontational, but has since been rivaled by the films of porn auteur Christopher Rage.

In a 1976 review of *Born to Raise Hell* (one assumes upon its rerelease), *Drummer* critic Sidney Charles notes the film "has something for everyone, including offense: its detractors are legion, alas, and in some circles it's the film you love to hate" (1976, p. 15). The filmmakers were obviously aware of the movie's contentious subject matter, for they prologued the film with a disclaimer, stating in part: "This theatre is not responsible for any psychological effects to the viewer." The outrage and controversy *Born to Raise Hell* was liable to incite led to the film's being cancelled in both Los Angeles and Atlanta. An interesting side note to this is that, although the film met with no controversy in San Francisco, to this day the state of California strictly prohibits the filmic representation of water sports and fistfucking. That this law is a direct consequence of the film's release is doubtful, though not impossible.

In its first phase, above-ground commercial gay porn relied heavily on the aesthetic tropes of the underground experimental gay cinema, partly for marketing purposes, and partly because the avant-garde heritage was an immediate and enduring influence on the new generation of filmmakers. Dyer draws attention to the structural similarities between the two genres: "Many of the structures of underground film, formal analogues of psychic states organise gay porn: dreams (*Song of the Loon* 1970, *Boys in the Sand*), memories (*Nights in Black Leather* 1972), hallucinogenic visions (*Destroying Angel* 1975), and conscious fantasising (*Boys in the Sand, American Cream* 1972), all always sexual, often intercut, Chinese boxed or not clearly distinguishable from one another" (1990, p. 171).

Many other gay porn films from the early 1970s reverently echo their underground predecessors. Among the more notable are: *Falconhead* (1972, Caballero/Vidco) directed by Michael Zen, which contemplates the surreal carnality experienced by homo-narcissists when lured through the looking glass by a falcon-headed body-builder; *Left-Handed* (1972, Hand in Hand) directed by Jack Deveau and Jaap Penraat, a love triangle narrative exploring the relationships among an antique dealer, his hustler boyfriend, and their drug dealer (who is married); and *That Boy* (1974, HIS Video) directed by and starring Peter Berlin, the sensitive story of Berlin befriending a young blind man. Berlin visualizes the erotic fantasies the blind man verbally relates but is unable to see (whether he is able to *visualize* them is unclear). The film is populated by many radical queer hippie types who appear to have looted the *Godspell* wardrobe room.

The current crop of gay porn has forsaken much of the artiness and aesthetic pretense in which the films of the early 1970s revelled, opting instead for minimal narrative and maximum sexual performance. But the early attempts at art-porn have not gone totally unrewarded. *Born to Raise Hell, L.A. Plays Itself, Sex Garage,* and *Sextool* have all been screened at the Museum of Modern Art in New York City. *L.A. Plays Itself, Sex Garage,* and a trailer for *Sextool* have all been honored with a position in the permanent film collection of the Museum, an honor most current gay porn releases are not likely to ever be awarded.*

The history of gay male pornography is fascinating in its wherewithal and complex in its chronology and breadth of homosexual imagery. Perhaps soon there will exist an expansive text which exhaustively time-lines the subject. Here, however, the focus is on that which is chronicled through gay porn, rather than on a further elaboration of the discursive and generalized overview of the genre presented in this chapter.

---

*According to Museum of Modern Art film archivist Robert Beers, the museum sponsored a Fred Halsted evening at which the Museum's film curator addressed the audience with the opening line: "Do you know what fistfucking is?" much to the chagrin of Catholic protesters in the streets.

Chapter III

Visions and Revisions

Although porn serves to document the sexual culture of gay men, it is not only the sex in these videos that will be addressed. It is the representations of the sites of sex and the accompanying roles which are among the most important aspects of this pornography. At the same time that porn, as a manifestation of gay male popular memory, captures the presence and existence of homosexual sex practices (historicizing them for future generations), it also actively rewrites American history. Gay male porn represents gay men in those sites and occupations in which we have always been, but in which we have mostly been invisible. These are sites and occupations which have, until very recently, existed solely under heterosexual male jurisdiction: the military (although we are currently attempting to change that), athletics, private industry, fraternities, the Wild West, law enforcement, politics, farms, prisons, and other hypermasculine occupations such as construction, plumbing, truck driving, and auto mechanics. I will return to this topic later. Since porn is fundamentally about sex, it is sex (or rather, the representations of sex) which I will discuss first.

THE SEXUAL EVOLUTION

Video pornography works in two ways. First, it serves to validate and legitimate homosexuality to the viewer. Second, by documenting the sexual and erotic trends and practices of gay men, pornography serves as a form of historiography. Richard Dyer, in "Coming to Terms," one of the first theoretical treatises on gay male porn, states:

Homosexual desire has been constructed as perverse and un-speakable; gay porn does speak/show gay sex. Gay porn as-serts homosexual desire, it turns the definition of homosexual desire on its head, says bad is good, sick is healthy and so on. It thus defends the universal human practice of same-sex physical contact (which our society constructs as homosexu-al); it has made life bearable for countless millions of gay men. (1985, p. 27)

Gay male porn merely reasserts that which gay men already know. But it always helps to know someone else is thinking and feeling the same things. In this regard, gay porn works in two ways. It reflects gay sexual practices, and, at the same time, constructs new erotic trends. Dyer terms this the "reeducation of desire" (Ibid.). That is to say, pornography, as a visual means of representation, usually elicits a physical response (orgasm) from the viewer, and therefore has the potential to educate the viewer about his body's sexual possibilities. Dyer's proposal here is intriguing, but rather incomplete. Within the body of this 1985 essay there is not a single mention of AIDS.* If ever there was an epochal epitome of the reeducation of desire, it is now, during the post-1980 AIDS crisis.

Therefore, in this analysis of gay pornographic sexual repre-sentations, it is necessary to divide the discussion into two sec-tions: homosexual sex, pre-AIDS awareness, and homosexual sex, AIDS awareness. It is important to note here that this analy-sis is conducted using a pornographist time-line, as opposed to a historical time-line. On the pornographist time-line, "pre-AIDS awareness" designates the period from 1970 to 1987, roughly. This is in contrast to the historical time-line which positions "pre-AIDS awareness" as any time prior to 1980.** Subsequent-ly, on the pornographist time-line, one finds that "AIDS aware-ness" (i.e., the practice of safe sex) begins around 1987. This discrepancy between time-lines is disturbing.

---

*"Still Alive in '85" was a popular battle cry at the time.
**Awareness of modes of viral transmission (and, therefore, awareness of safer sex techniques) occurs, roughly, in the period after 1982.

Pre-AIDS Awareness

In the 1982 video *Heatstroke* (HIS Video), there is an orgy sequence featuring Casey Donovan. During this scene, Donovan anally and orally services a number of different men (most of whose faces are never visible). Two outstanding examples of sex from this sequence: 1. Donovan gives a blow job to an African-American. The man ejaculates onto his own hand and Donovan's face. The man wipes Donovan's face with his cum-stained hand, then shoves his hand down Donovan's throat. Donovan sucks it up, happily and hungrily. 2. Donovan gives a blow job to Clinton Coe (whose face the viewer does see). Coe ejaculates into Donovan's mouth. The viewer knows that Coe has achieved orgasm because Donovan then stands up and spews Coe's ejaculate onto and into Coe's open mouth. The two then French kiss. Donovan licks the remainder of Coe's ejaculate from Coe's face.

Another example, from *The Bigger the Better* (1984, Falcon): Buster and Mike Ramsey, in a hotel room bed, reciprocally suck and fuck each other. When Buster fucks Ramsey, he pulls out, ejaculates, then reinserts his penis up Ramsey's butt, using the sperm as lubricant.

Both *Heatstroke* and *The Bigger the Better* are typical examples of pre-AIDS awareness porn's treatment of homosexual sex. It is not much different from porn produced before 1980 (the real era of pre-AIDS awareness) except for the fact that the production values are much higher and they were originally shot on video as opposed to eight- or 16-millimeter film. In the 1970s the above sexual expressions were de rigueur. In the 1980s and 1990s they are, of course, potentially fatal. In the period before gay male porn chose to recognize AIDS, any and every sexual act was acceptable. The anonymity granted by orgies and glory-holes diffused the possibilities of emotional connection and dependence. On the other hand, acts like Donovan and Coe's cum-swapping kiss are highly charged in an interpersonally emotional sense.

In gay male video's first heyday (1972-1982), all levels of gay male experience were pornographic material. *A Night at Halsted's* (1982, HIS Video) documents the anonymous sexual encounters that take place one evening in a Los Angeles leather bar. *L.A. Tool*

& Die (1979, HIS Video) is the story of an unrequited love, in which Richard Locke follows the man of his dreams across the country. They eventually live happily ever after. In those halcyon exploratory days of the celebration of the more open and free gay lifestyle, all levels of erotic experience were faithfully documented by the porn industry. For gay men who were just coming out, these films offered a plethora of sexual possibilities; they were how-to manuals for the novice. Gay porn celebrated the gay lifestyle in which men could be whores, men could be monogamous, or men could cruise the spectrum in between.

Somewhere around 1982, however, the industry changed. The advent of video and the creation of the home viewing market made gay male porn a big business. AIDS, too, began to take its toll. The epidemic was quickly working its way into the American consciousness. The coincidence of these two factors greatly affected the state of gay male pornography.

Until the advent of the home video market, the participants (performers, directors, crew) in gay male porn were mostly there for their own sexual gratification. Recently deceased porn actor and director Al Parker claims to have began his career as a model with Colt Studios primarily to meet other men with similar exhibitionistic interests (1990). Granted, these performers were paid; but most were involved in order to explore new sexual freedoms. When gay video became big business, the filmmakers became money moguls, and the concept of porn stars developed into a full-blown star system. The industry became more depersonalized and image-oriented, and the videos reflect this change. In the vanguard of this "new wave" in gay porn production were directors Matt Sterling and John Travis, among others. Both accrued substantial wealth in other businesses and were able to make the first "big budget" videos (Parker 1990).

Backed by ample budgets, Sterling and Travis were able to afford the latest in video technology and production values, as well as prime models. The objects of these directors' erotic desires are young, muscular, "straight-looking" guys. Through the lures of money and potential fame, Sterling and Travis employed many straight performers for their videos: "gay for pay," as it is known in the trade. The atypical sexual preferences of this new breed of porn performers is clearly evident in the films of that period (1982-1988). There is no longer that feeling of discovery, freedom, and sexual abandon one gets from watching Casey Donovan and Al Parker get it on together. Performing in porn flicks is now less an extension of one's sexual desires than it is a profession, craft, and quick source of under-the-table income.

Consequently, the sex acts in this period of videos change. The cum-swapping French kiss and reciprocal butt-fuck are no longer the standard procedures. The straight stars receive most of the servicing. Reciprocity is at a minimum and only exists in an attempt to half-heartedly convince the viewer that these guys are enjoying themselves. A 30-second quasi-blow job with the eyes closed is the most that can be expected from these "gay for pay" boys. But one can hardly expect straight men in need of fast money to be capable of convincing the camera (and the viewer) that emotional and erotic bonds exist between them and their partners. These men are not actors and these men are not gay.

In fact, a hierarchicalization of porn stars begins to occur within the star system. This hierarchy, vanguarded by Travis and Sterling, positions straight-identified actors such as Rick Donovan, Brian Maxon, Tony Stefano, Tim Lowe, Matt Ramsey, and Tom Brock–men who, infrequently, could get fucked for bucks, but would not be caught dead swallowing semen or kissing a buddy on the lips–at the top, and usually in the top's position, while the more obviously "gay" performers (i.e., bottoms who enjoy being penetrated) are given a lesser status. Straight men who perform in gay porn are considered a rare commodity and are therefore considered by many as worthy of a higher adoration than the more common gay actor. Author Tom Kalin marks 1982 as the beginning of a similar trend of visual representation in mainstream media. Kalin traces the advent of this trend to the first homoerotic Calvin Klein underwear ads photographed by Bruce Weber:

> It was in Andy Warhol's *Interview* (long-time flesh market-place) and other similar magazines that Bruce Weber's vision of the unattainable, eroticized male first appeared, "fine art" advertising sponsored by the conglomerate Calvin Klein. Ironically, at a time when homophobia was on the rise, Weber,

Warhol, and Klein were able to cunningly sell homoerotic imagery to a mass audience. Yet this was a most complicated homoeroticism, it was–contradiction of contradictions–a deeply conservative, homophobic homoeroticism. Klein and Weber exploit their male models' presumed heterosexuality and "natural" masculine beauty. Usually athletes and working class men partially unclothed, their public semi-nudity is excused via accepted cultural modes of male bonding. Free to titillate on the forbidden edge between football's ass-patting and lovers' caresses, these invincible, unattainable members of the master race (always white, often blonde) act as perfect mannequins, able, even in underwear, to remain both fully eroticized and socially clothed. (1992, p. 125)

Gay pornography also fell victim to this same trend of homophobic homoerotica. The performers, especially the straight-identified ones, and the directors, successfully replicated the mainstream norm. (To this date, Calvin Klein underwear remains the underwear of choice in these videos.) The straight-identified actors of this period mimic the qualities of being unattainable and invincible that Kalin astutely projects onto Weber's models. Even when they give over to the animal urge of fucking a hole, even if it belongs to another man, they never let on that such an act is typical of their behavior. The other man is never given the satisfaction of attainment; he has been attained unreciprocally. There are few instances in which two straight-identified men meet. When they do, and one is sexually vanquished by the other, it is still understood that their hetero-masculinity has not been violated. The two men each honor the other's unattainability and invincibility, regardless of what has just transpired. The sex comes and goes without ever being intimately approached or romantically embraced. Weber's images of homoerotic bonding have merely been played out to their pornographic extreme; the inherent homophobia, however, has been left intact.

This particular wave of video succeeds primarily documenting the fact that video sex had turned into a capitalist venture. Gay sex sells, whether it be videos or underwear, and straight porn performers have learned to exploit this.

In terms of AIDS this same period is full of denial. The porn industry's denial of the epidemic's existence, however, did nothing in the way of placating the paranoia and hatred it instilled in people. Astoundingly, as late as 1988 most gay porn videos were not incorporating safe sex techniques. Then again, safe sex as a nationwide movement did not really gain full momentum until 1987, the year the AIDS Coalition to Unleash Power (ACT UP) was formed.

Gay pornographers in the two-year interim following 1985 had probably not read Richard Dyer's essay, and were uninformed of the fact that porn could function as a possible site for the reeducation of desire. In retrospect, the nonexistence of safe sex representations in gay porn during this period does more to reflect the fear and denial embodied by the industry than it does to document the erotic trends of the time.

Gay pornography of the mid- to late 1980s is a strange sexual hybrid. Gay men were leaving the business due to illness, fear, and even death (one of the first gay stars to die of AIDS was Dave Connors, in 1985), or else they were being made obsolete by the top directors in the industry who could afford to fetishize and homoeroticize straight men. AIDS was wreaking physical and psychic havoc on the country, instilling a wave of denial in most people–especially among straight men who were convinced that they could not or would not contract it. This wave of AIDS-denying straight young men proliferating throughout gay porn explains why the type of sex represented in these videos changed so drastically. This period of video saw the disappearance of such personal and emotionally charged acts as cum-swallowing and French kissing, but yet did not demonstrate an understanding of the necessity for safe sex practices. Anal and oral intercourse occurred impersonally without condoms.

In 1985 *Lifeguard* (HIS Video), the first safe-sex video, was produced. Unfortunately it was not very well made, either technically or erotically, and consequently went by unnoticed. The sex scenes in *Lifeguard* are devoted solely to practices which do not involve the exchange of bodily fluids. Anal sex does not occur because in 1985 it was still not known if condom usage prevented transmission of HIV (Rowberry 1990, p. 158). The video also does very little in the way of eroticizing safe sex practices. The men involved perform under the hierarchical privileging of the straight-identified actors.

In retrospect, the gay pornography produced between 1983 and 1988 mostly reflects a job devoid of sexual pleasure, a manifestation of gay cultural popular memory discouragingly smattered with ego-dystonic homosexuality and AIDS-phobia.

AIDS Awareness

Nineteen eighty-seven marks the beginning of a significant shift in the erotic representations in gay male videos. It is not too much of a stretch to see the correlation between this shift and the shift in gay and AIDS activism which occurred with the formation of ACT UP. Gay pride in an angry and militant manifestation (as opposed to the more hedonistic form it took in the 1970s) was forcing its way into the American consciousness. Condoms were forcing their way into the American consciousness as well. As implements of safe sex, condoms became the center of much political rhetoric. And slowly their use infiltrated the fantasy realms of gay pornography. Although there are still some straight-identified porn stars in the industry (Rex Chandler, Lex Baldwin, and Matt Powers being among the most successful), the trend has turned back toward enthusiastically queer performers who enjoy each other's sexual company (French kissing in particular has made a huge comeback in videos of the 1990s).

At first, condoms were used very surreptitiously in these videos. In these late 1980s, early 1990s AIDS-aware films, footage involving the application of the rubbers is usually edited. Also edited are initial scenes of anal penetration (especially close-ups). What the viewer sees is two men in the midst of anal intercourse. Subsequent close-up shots of penetration usually reveal that the fucker is wearing a rubber. Again, for the climax shot, the magic of editing makes the condom disappear: the topman pulls out, sans rubber, and shoots his load onto the bottom's back, butt, face, or chest. Condoms and their application have not, for the most part, been successfully eroticized, contrary to prevalent gay male practice in real life.

To date there are only two films of which I know that utilize condoms during oral sex scenes: *On the Rocks* (1990, Stryker Productions) and *Turbo Charge* (1988, Surge Studios/Vidco). *On the*

Rocks is particularly interesting for a number of reasons, the most important being the kinky variation on the safe sex theme in the scene leading up to the blow job-with-rubber. A young guy (unlisted in the credits) is alone in a porn producer's office, watching a video of gay porn superstar Jeff Stryker. Stryker strips, talks dirty, and masturbates for the viewer (in this case, both the actor and the home viewer). The young guy, turned on by Stryker's video, strips and masturbates as well. Eventually he decides he needs to get fucked. But there is nobody around to oblige him. So he fucks himself with his own dick. Jeff Stryker himself then walks into the office, unannounced, and sees the guy performing auto-intercourse, as it were. Stryker gets turned on and asks the guy if he wants to suck some dick while fucking himself. The guy, of course, does. But first he applies a condom to Stryker's dick, excitedly emphasizing "for safe sex." What follows is one of the best examples of the eroticization of condom application in gay porn. The guy forms an "O" with his mouth, then lightly places the condom into the space. Stryker then inserts his penis into the open end of the condom, while the guy uses his tongue, teeth, lips, and throat to roll the rubber down the length of the shaft. This accomplished, the typical blow job ensues.

This particular example is by no means the norm in current gay video, either in terms of the eroticization of the condom application, or the use of condoms during oral sex. Fortunately, the use of condoms during anal intercourse is now standard procedure. There has been much contestation in the science and medical professions concerning the dangers of unprotected oral sex. The current belief is that so long as the ejaculate is not ingested, there is probably minimal risk of contracting HIV. It is also believed that certain chemicals in saliva and in the stomach kill the virus, thereby decreasing the risk of infection through the ingestion of pre-seminal fluid. In porn videos, ejaculate is never directly ingested due to the convenient pornographic trope of the "cum shot" in which the penetrator withdraws in order that the camera may record the orgasm. Therefore, cum, when ingested in these films, has usually been exposed to oxygen. It is a widely held belief that such exposure kills the HIV virus.

The above scene between Jeff Stryker and the safe sex enthusiast exemplifies another current trend in AIDS-aware gay porn: auto-erotica. In this age of AIDS, when many men are choosing to stay home and avoid sexual contact altogether (abstinence as safe sex), a plethora of solo jack-off scenes (and, indeed, videos) has come into existence. Although the above porn star's auto-erotic experience was interrupted by Stryker, numerous other examples of guys getting off on their own bodies exist. Buckshot's Minute Man Video Series (a division of Colt Studio) is dedicated to representations of hot men erotically and lovingly masturbating and enjoying the feel of their own bodies.

The Minute Man videos tend to be one hour long, and consist of four 15-minute sequences, each presenting a different muscle-bound man. The scenes usually incorporate exhibitionistic full-body sensuality: the stroking of muscles, pinching of nipples, exposing of the anus for the viewer, and masturbation culminating in orgasm. These videos reflect the somewhat disheartening trend of abstinence within the gay community. But in doing so, they maximize the effect to its full erotic potential. They are about people who stay home and masturbate watching somebody else who has decided to stay home and masturbate.

There are many other good examples of auto-erotic pornography. The video *Blow Your Own Horn* (1989, Vivid) showcases guys capable of auto-fellatio. And *Hin Yin For Men: Ancient Secrets of Relaxation and Self-Eroticism* (1990, Lost Angel), directed by Thomas Mitchell, a New Age self-help how-to porn video, was advertised in handouts thus:

> Loving another starts & ends with acts and decisions to love oneself . . . HIN YIN is an old Chinese term for the "private parts"–the genitals, perineum, and the anus. Three models demonstrate age-old erotic practices virtually unknown in the West, including anal and penile massage . . . in this ground-breaking, taboo-shattering, instructional video.

Alternative solo erotic techniques are exemplified in other videos by actors Joey Stefano and Damien who, whether solo or accompanied, often ingest their own ejaculate. There are also numerous scenes in gay porn videos of men fucking themselves with dildos in the absence of a partner–or perhaps in preference over a partner. The fact that gay men are becoming more and more sexually self-reliant is one of the consequences of the AIDS epidemic. That they have been successful, and will continue to be so, is evidenced in their pornography, which both reflects these changing attitudes and helps construct new methods and variations on the masturbation theme.

It is interesting to note the evolution of representations of safe sex in gay male video pornography in relation to the evolution of the politicization of AIDS. In the first years of the epidemic's spread, AIDS was constructed by moral majoritarians and right-wing politicians as a tool to be used against the marginal communities it first struck: gay men and intravenous drug users. The sense of fear and even self-hatred these politicians instilled in the gay community in particular, in regard to their sex, evidenced itself in the culture's pornography. Most of the sexual practices that gay men had enjoyed during the 1970s appeared in modified form in these videos, without the same elan or abandon. Sexual promiscuity (i.e., multiple partners) was laid to blame. But sexual promiscuity and freedom were part of the point of gay sexual liberation. So sexual promiscuity continued to characterize the narratives of gay porn, only now it did so with a grimace.

In the late 1980s, a counter-politicization of AIDS by gay-positive groups began to take shape. Gay Men's Health Crisis (GMHC), which had actually been in existence since 1982 but only really gained wide recognition when its founder, Larry Kramer, left to organize the more militant ACT UP, as well as the groups ACT UP and Queer Nation, refused the New Right's abuse of AIDS as a demonizing construct. Through demonstrations, guerrilla art, meetings, and safe sex workshops, these groups helped the gay community rethink its position in this society, and forced this society to rethink its position in relation to gay and other minority cultures. In "How to Have Promiscuity in an Epidemic" Douglas Crimp points out that gay men, able to recognize that AIDS is no fault of sexual promiscuity, use the knowledge sexual promiscuity affords to extend their bodily awareness and to learn new and safer sex techniques:

> We were able to invent safe sex because we have always
> known that sex is not, in an epidemic or not, limited to pene-
> trative sex. Our promiscuity taught us many things, not only
> about the pleasures of sex, but about the great multiplicity of
> those pleasures. It is that psychic preparation, that exper-
> imentation, that conscious work on our own sexualities that
> has allowed many of us to change our sexual behaviors . . .
> very quickly and very dramatically . . . *it is our promiscuity
> that will save us.* (1987, p. 253)

As a result, we are now witnessing a distinct attitude adjustment
in the most current of gay male porn videos. Promiscuity and multiple sex partners are still within the sexual repertoire. But now, for
the most part, they follow safe sex guidelines. Even when the fantasy of certain scenarios should definitely not call for safe sex, it is
employed nonetheless. In *Lunch Hour* (1990, Catalina) there is a
dream sequence in which a group of disgruntled factory employees
with inadvertent Marxist tendencies rapes the oppressive manage-
ment team. And they use condoms–an unlikely precautionary discipline for rapists, real or dreamed. This points to an intriguing reshaping of the gay community's sexual psyche: in our daydreams
and sexual imaginings–mine, and those of many others I know as
well–safe sex is a very present factor.

I put forth, to cultural anthropologists, ethnographers, and any-
one else interested in studying the gay male communities, that those
communities' video pornography is an important indicator of this
culture's seemingly hidden sexual history. The trends in sexual
practice, whether physical or psychical, are clearly manifest in these
erotic films. With apologies for the generalities, I have illustrated
the birth and evolution of these pornographic representations and
their relation, whether constructive, reflective, or both, to the actual
practice of the sex. The study of these sexual representations in
conjunction with a broader cultural and social analysis is very telling and, indeed, vital to the understanding of the contemporary
American history of gay men.

BEYOND SEX

Beyond the practice of man-to-man sex there is another vital aspect of pornographic representations of the gay male. These are representations of the gay men themselves: their look, their attire, their attitudes, and their situations in space and time. In a much less obvious way, these images are also very important to the construction and representation of the history of gay men. Whereas the sexual acts in these videos serve as indicators of sexual preference, it is the presentation of self (or character) and location which situate gay men in their greater historical context.

Re-Writing the Past

In recent years there has been a great increase in academic writings focusing on gay and lesbian history. Among the more notable are *Hidden From History: Reclaiming the Gay and Lesbian Past*, edited by Martin Duberman, Martha Vicinus, and George Chauncey, Jr., and *Coming Out Under Fire*, by Allan Bérubé. These books and others are important and illuminating steps forward in the gay communities' attempts to rewrite both American and world history; but their limited accessibility is unfortunate. In the words of the Popular Memory Group:

> For the modern period there is a real problem of the implicitly non-popular effects of focusing on formal history-writing, a practice largely colonized by academic and professional norms . . . If we retain this focus, we risk reproducing some very conservative forms: a closed circle of comment between left social historians and what Marx would have called 'critical critics' . . . 'Two observable trends' that might account for this: the concentration of history in higher education . . . and the expense of commercially published books. (1982, p. 206)

The standards of historiography have always been set by the people with the better educations and higher incomes. These standards, however, exclude a great many people from the pursuit of knowledge. Books like Bérubé's are very often not available to people not living near metropolitan or university centers. Indeed, even those people located near such centers may not have access to such books simply because they do not know such books exist. In response to this dilemma, the Popular Memory Group insists upon "the need to expand the idea of historical production well beyond the limits of academic history-writing" (Ibid., p. 207).

I suggest that gay male porn videos are examples of history writing beyond the limits of academia. By no means is this history writing a necessarily conscious effort on the part of the pornographers. In fact, most of it is completely inadvertent. Nonetheless, these videos do serve as history texts of the gay male experience in two ways. First, many of them resituate gay men into past and present social conditions in which they have always been, but in which they have mostly been hidden (such as the California gold rush, the U.S. Armed Forces, and college fraternities). Second, the videos also document current gay-specific social conditions, such as bar life, nightclubs, bathhouses, and so on. Inadvertence, again, is a key issue here, because most of gay porn's viewing audience is probably unaware of the historical and political ramifications of what they are seeing. It is hard, however, to imagine that an 18-year-old gay male today, viewing Al Parker's *Turned On*, would be fully unaware of the indirect gay history lesson he is receiving by watching the sexual escapades that took place in that now mostly defunct social phenomenon, the gay bathhouse.

For the purposes of this book I will give a brief two-part overview of the predominant trends in gay video porn from the perspective of nonacademic history writing. The first part will focus on what this society has constructed as straight male-specific sites and roles, both past and present, and gay men's situation within them. Although the videos' representations of this are by no means always accurate or authentic, they do capture the unique "take" on western history many gay men enjoy. The second part will deal primarily with gay-specific sites and roles. I will then put forth some preliminary conclusions regarding the juncture of the history of erotics and erotics as history as evidenced in gay male video pornography.

It is not much of a secret to gay men that gay men were present in the days of Caligula, Emperor of Rome (reign: A.D. 37-41). They were most certainly around before this period too, but in terms of pornographic representations of gay male history, this is one of the earliest epochs these videos address. *Centurians of Rome* (1981, Hand in Hand), directed by John Christopher, is the love story of two Roman slaves (George Payne and Scorpio). They are forcefully separated early in the film; Payne is delivered to Caligula as a sex-toy, and Scorpio becomes the love interest of a Roman guard. After many sexual exploits, including a dirty-talk fistfuck delivered to Caligula by Payne, the two slaves are reunited.

Gay men were also around during the European Renaissance. Jean-Daniel Cadinot's film *Carnival in Venice* (1987, Talk of the Town) is an updated gay retelling of the story of Romeo and Juliet. Here, Romeo and Julien (a spoiled French boy vacationing in Venice) fall into each others arms after the Carnival masquerade, several bawdy adventures, and an introduction into a secret sexual society. Unlike Shakespeare's doomed heterosexuals, Romeo and Julien enjoy a more upbeat finale.

Another not so well-kept secret is that homosexual males abounded in the days of the exploratory expansion of America's western frontier. There are many porn videos which rewrite these pages of America's history incorporating gay men into the action. The classic soft-core *Song of the Loon* (1969, Studio 1 Amusements), *In Hot Pursuit* (1987, Catalina), *Cowboys and Indians* (1989, Vivid Video), and *Gold Rush Boys* (1981, Jocks Athletic Co.) are all good examples. Outstanding among these Wild West videos, however, is Frank Jeffries's *Northwest Passage* (1987, Adam & Company). This video incorporates a "story within a story" narrative formula: a trucker relates to a young hitchhiker the love story of a frontier cartographer (loosely based on Lewis Meriwether) and an Indian brave. The American frontier is beautifully photographed, and the antagonistic and genocidal relationship between the white man and the Native American is given an idyllic twist in the form of a sensitive and delicate homosexual love affair. *Northwest Passage* is a revisionist Western beyond the imaginative scope of Robert Altman or Sam Peckinpah; not only does it positively situate gay men in a hyper-heterosexual atmosphere, the video also poses an altruistic "what if" hypothesis: what if more well-adjusted gay men had been sent into the frontier? Perhaps, this film suggests, clearly without basis, that public relations between the white man and the Native American might not be so destructive.

In the America of the 1950s gay men were notoriously hidden behind the fantasy facade of the *Leave it to Beaver* model of the nuclear family. Even in the ultra male domains of *The Wild One* and *Rebel Without a Cause* homoeroticism was kept at bay by a benevolent yet sexual Natalie Wood-type heroine. As a vision of the 1950s, Patrick Dennis's *Davey and the Cruisers* (1989, Vivid Video) is to gay adult video what *Grease* was to Broadway and Hollywood musicals. *Davey and the Cruisers* is about car clubs (The Cruisers), soda shops, and high school hoodlum mechanics. The protagonist, Davey, is a certifiable nerd who wants to become a Cruiser. By means of cocksucking and anal-receptive sex, he succeeds in doing so. This video puts forth that the *real* cool dudes of the 1950s were the well-adjusted queer boys, taking full advantage of the homosocial environment provided by exclusive clubs and gangs. These boys take the homoerotic tension between Marlon Brando and Lee Marvin one step further. Also notable in this 1950s sub-genre is *Cruisin' '57* (1979, Bijou Video), which weaves together several unrelated episodes concerning 1950s rock-and-rollers.

An unpleasant epoch of American history, and one that seems an unlikely choice in which pornographers might situate the homoerotic experience, is the Vietnam War. *Foxhole* (1989, Catalina) by John Travis does just that. In a camouflage tent, near a battlefront, a GI writes letters home to his fuck-buddy detailing the sexual exploits of his platoon compatriots. The seriousness and perversity of the war is subsumed by the well-produced erotic interludes in this film. Outdoor showers, demanding commanding officers, medical exams, and even the dangerous vulnerability of the foxhole are all imbued with a heavy erotic aura. Here again, American society's penchant for creating homosocial environments explodes into a gay orgy of pleasure and romance. The hippie slogan "Make Love, Not War" is carried to the front lines of literalness: in *Foxhole* war can wait; love and sex come first. Even in the foxhole itself, a locale rife with wartime sensibilities, love seems to prevail; it deters enemy attack. The sensual and ecstatic experiences of homosexual sex override the severity of the war. These life-affirming, gay-affirming acts in the midst of fear and fatality serve to better highlight the obscenity of the war. In comparison, society's construct of homosexuality (and for that matter, pornography or any form of sexuality) as an obscenity appears ludicrous in the face of the American experience in Vietnam.

The above genre of gay male video pornography serves as a revisionist history for the gay community: these films are one-handed histories focusing on the gay experience in major world events and epochs. They are revisionist in the same way that texts like *Coming Out Under Fire* or *Hidden From History* are revisionist: they all expose, assert, and celebrate the presence of gay men (and, in the case of the books, lesbians) in history. The socially imposed invisibility of the gay communities is considerably undermined by these new avenues in historiography. This is accomplished in a dual manner: first, by proclaiming the very existences of gay communities, and second, by proclaiming their existence within the primarily heterosexual domain of historiography.

Although pornography, as a radical rewriting of history, may not directly confront or affront the hegemonic social order, it does serve its community well. Most straight people (men in particular) have very little occasion or desire to view gay male porn videos. Gay men, on the other hand, usually have considerable experience with these videos. Because they are easily accessed via video rental outlets, magazine advertisements, and metropolitan gay cinemas, these films reach a substantial portion of the gay community. In fact, even areas assumed to be untouched by the commercial spread of gay porn are not: Oklahoma, for instance, is reputedly the state with the strongest mail-order gay porn market (Waugh 1985, p. 33).

In other words, these gay revisionist histories, delivered in a pornographic context, substantially alter the way most gay men perceive American history. These videos do not necessarily imply authenticity or facticity. That is, the viewer does not really believe that it was a common occurrence in 1950s suburban America for soda shop drag queens to fanatically chase after the members of a gay car club. Gertrude Koch, speaking primarily of straight pornography and its male consumers, suggests that "pornography does not so much express dominant male sexual practice as it expresses its deficiencies, restructuring damaged fantasies" (1990, p. 26). A key deficiency suffered by the gay communities is that, until recently, the historicization of gay men has indeed been a "damaged fantasy." These videos, then, deconstruct the oppressing standards of

orthodox history. They parody the norm, and consequently instill in
the gay male viewer himself the ability to question that which is
presented as authentic history. These videos are reparative. They
make room for new historic truths, whether these be the ones they
proffer or ones the viewer invents on his own. As a subject of study,
this genre of porn video documents the satiric slant the gay community has on the issue of American history. We know where we were
(and are), but until we are allowed access to the more mainstream
forms of representation, we will take full advantage of the more
marginal means, such as pornography and academic texts.

Re-Writing the Present: Men at Work

The Popular Memory Group asserts that for full and inclusive
historic representation, we must become "historians of the present
too" (1982, p. 205). Another genre of gay male porn video helps
serve this purpose. In this genre, videos construct sites and roles
most usually associated with heterosexual men, and then populates them
with gay men. *The Adam Film World 1991 Directory: Gay Adult Video*
gives a breakdown of over 1,000 gay videos by "theme." Included
among these themes are many examples of stereotypically heterosexual male sites and roles: athletes (71 videos), construction workers
(27), cops (19), cowboys (15), detectives (5), exercise and health
clubs (6), farms and farmers (6), garage and mechanics (9), medical
(9), military (17), movers and haulers (5), office sex (4), plumbers
(2), prison (13), repairmen (9), restaurants (4), sports (17), students
(30), surfers (9), and uniforms (25). This list, of course, is not complete. There are many videos (and thus themes) which the *Directory*
does not cover. Also, some of the videos included display a certain
degree of mutability among themes. *One in a Billion* (1984, Vidco),
for example, includes a variety of different characters and locales,
and so is listed under both the themes of "office sex" and "repairmen." However, most instances of multithematic videos are not so
diligently categorized; many are omitted entirely from the publication's theme section.

In most of the above social roles and conditions, it is professional
(and perhaps physical) suicide to avow one's homosexuality.
Construction workers, cops, truckers, and the like are not supposed
to be gay. In American society, these are manly occupations, and

gays, by convention, are not "manly." Of course this is a pure myth of gender. For the longest time women were not supposed to be construction workers, cops, or truckers either. That both gay men and women exist in these areas is unquestionable. Gay men, however, are easily made invisible by the social structure. By means of gender, they can "pass" as straight men. "Passing" may be enforced for personal safety, or by one's co-workers' refusal to recognize the issue. Gay porn videos cut through these gender rules and enforced silences and offer gay men a vision of free expression of their sexual desires in these locales.

One of the earliest porn examples of gay men in "straight" roles (not including the hetero-fetishism of the earlier physique films) is the 1971 film *Pink Narcissus*. The film, as discussed earlier, is not a typical hardcore porn flick; there are lots of butt shots, fleeting glimpses of veiled hard-ons and fully exposed flaccid penises, simulated fellatio, and one cum shot (that may only be a special effect). The narrative is built around the daydreams of a narcissistic young boy who imagines himself in many sexual encounters with random men. The final scene of the movie is set in a post-apocalyptic metropolis populated by seminude gay men. All of these men don traditionally straight male costumes: the cop, the sailor, the marine, the construction worker, and even a Davey Crockett-like frontiersman. The costumes are designed so that the genitals are always exposed. This allows the men to masturbate and flaunt their meat for the others. In the city streets of *Pink Narcissus* heterosexual costuming is appropriated and recoded into a gay sexual language by gay men. But perhaps "appropriated" is the wrong word, for these examples of "heterosexual costuming" are part of the American male legacy as a whole–gay or straight. The dominant social order has merely constructed these roles and their respective outfits as heterosexual. In reality, such clothing is worn by men of all sexual persuasions. Such professions are practiced by men of all sexual persuasions. In everyday life, the gay presence in these realms has been silenced. Gay male pornography breaks that silence, speaks their presence, and allows gay men their right to exist in whatever capacity they wish.

Other superior examples of gay porn videos which make gay men visible in places where they have mostly been invisible include the Joe Gage working man trilogy, which consists of *Kansas City Trucking Co.* (1976, HIS Video), *El Paso Wrecking Corp.* (1977, HIS Video), and *L.A. Tool & Die* (1979, HIS Video). As their titles suggest, these videos are about gay men in the trucking and heavy machinery businesses. Homoeroticism slips out of the closet and into the gravel pits, truck stops, and work sites of America. Phrases like "wide load," "heavy load," "men at work," and "2x4" take on new meanings in these videos. A big rig trucker doesn't get much rest at a rest stop in Gage's all-male world.

One final interesting example from this genre of video is *Sizing Up* (1984, Huge Video). This film documents the athletic and sexual exploits of Olympic track and field contenders. Pregame and postgame romantic interludes are strung together with footage of the stars trying their best at the pole vault and discus throw. These actors fare much better when dealing with pole vaulting and discus throwing euphemistically. What does matter about this film is that it allows and even endorses athleticism (in its highest manifestation) in gay men. To take this one step further, of the relationship between homosexuality, pornography, and sports, Brian Pronger states:

> The ironic process of destruction and reconstruction is at work in all masculine homoerotic happenings. The homoerotic attraction for athletes takes the orthodox masculinity of athletes and, in a process of ironic deconstruction, violates that masculinity, reconstructing it as paradoxical masculinity. This is almost invariably the text of gay athletic porn: a situation that in the beginning seems to be heterosexual and masculine, by virtue of its athletic setting, turns out to be homosexual. (1990)

Similarly, Leo Bersani, in his article "Is the Rectum a Grave?" states:

> I want to propose, instead of a denial of what I take to be important (if politically unpleasant) truths about male homosexual desire, an arduous representational discipline. The sexist power that defines maleness in most human cultures can easily survive social revolutions; what it perhaps cannot survive is a certain way of assuming, or taking on, that power. If,

as [Jeffrey] Weeks puts it, gay men "gnaw at the roots of a male heterosexual identity," it is not because of the parodistic distance that they take from that identity, but rather because, from within their nearly mad identification with it, *they never cease to feel the appeal of its being violated.* (1987, p. 209)

Both Pronger and Bersani write of the desire gay men have for violating the heterosexist construct of masculinity. This need to violate it, according to Bersani, stems from gay men's "nearly mad identification with it." Nearly mad, of course, because gay men have always identified with it, always been a part of it, but have never been allowed to admit their homosexuality within its boundaries. The above genre of pornography serves as an erotic violation of this heterosexist masculine identity. Gay men desire to violate the power structure that is consuming their visibility. Gay men have always been in the locker rooms and the armed forces, but they have also always been invisible there. Video pornography allows these men to debunk the masculinist myths of homosexual inferiority by placing gay men back into these sites, and overpowering them with homoerotic impulses and desires. That athletes and commanding officers, usually considered to be straight, turn out to be gay (in pornography) deconstructs orthodox truths and allows them to be replaced by paradoxical potentials.

The sexual act is one of the most important ways in which homosexuality can make itself visible. Pornography practices this theory, at the expense of heterosexism and the social myth of gender. Gay pornography shows the *homoerotic* leaking into everyday reality–offices, gyms, rodeos, wherever. Further, it shows the *reality of homosexuality* leaking into everyday reality (read orthodox reality). Gay pornography layers truth upon half-truth. By homosexualizing such all-male conditions, these videos actively violate masculinist norms and deconstruct oppressive social standards. Cocksuckers in 18-wheelers, buttfuckers in the Olympics, and pit-sniffers in the police academy are merely hypereroticized representations of everyday truths. But they must be hypereroticized to combat and overcompensate for the severe degree of homosexual invisibility and marginalization.

* * *

What is the political relevance of this particular genre of gay male pornography? What is the political relevance of history, whether disseminated through adult videos or academic texts? One approach to the political relevance of history, suggests the Popular Memory Group,

> seeks to link past and present in the form of salutary 'lessons.' These may have a negative force, warning, for instance, against returns to past disasters . . . More generally still . . . the re-creation of popular struggles shows us that despite retreats and defeats, 'the people,' 'the working class,' or the female sex *do* 'make history' even under conditions of oppression or exploitation. In the same way, especially if we are conscious of this lineage, *we* can make history too. The link between the past and present, between history writing and the construction of historical futures today, is in essence an exhortatory one. (1982, p. 212)

It is interesting to look at the five examples of "porn-as-rewriting-history" discussed earlier. Each of them situates gay men in relatively bleak, frightening, or antagonistic places and times. But, as mentioned earlier in the discussion of *Northwest Passage*, the presence of gay men in these periods or situations adds a redemptive flair to otherwise pernicious and hateful atmospheres. These videos posit the presence of well-adjusted gay men in any environment (past, present, or future) as an asset. In the "theme" videos, the presence of gay men in certain sites and roles makes more positive the normally heterosexist, masculinist qualities of these places. These videos are exhortatory. They demand social equality for the gay communities. They encourage the creation of homosexual utopias. They position gay men as the only positive influence in otherwise abhorrent situations: Romeo and Julien can live happily ever after because, unlike Romeo and Juliet, they do not follow the prejudicial and destructive mandates of "family values." Loyalty to family, and procreation thereof, is not an issue for these two boys in love. They are able to move beyond it in their neo-Renaissance world. We here should be able to do the same.

Recording the Past

To return to the concept of history writing: there is another genre of gay male porn video which serves as cultural document (as opposed to sexual document). These are the videos whose action is set in contemporary homosexual utopias: gay bars, bathhouses, gay resorts, and gay events like the Gay Games. Although these videos, for the most part, were not intended to document the cultural prevalence and relevance of such locales, they nonetheless have done so, and can be studied as documents of the communities.

Of special interest in this genre are films which document the now-extinct gay social phenomena of bathhouses and the Greenwich Village piers. Both the bathhouses and the piers are fine examples of gay male sexual lifestyle in the 1970s and early 1980s. The piers were razed for zoning reasons, and bathhouses across the country closed for "health" reasons.* For the most part, the only extant visual documentation of these social and sexual spaces is in pornography.

Steve Scott's *Turned On* (1982, Le Salon) is as close a pornographic film comes to being an ethnographic documentary. Filmed on location in San Francisco's Club Baths, *Turned On* is now a historic cultural artifact. The makers of this film alerted the bathhouse patrons of their presence, and recruited many of the men to cooperate sexually. The architectural arrangement and the social and sexual life of the baths–the glory hole, the sauna, the shower room, the live stage show, the lockers, and the activities of the patrons–are presented explicitly.**

Turned On also documents an excellent example of high-caliber live stage performance. Actor Scott Taylor sweats and gyrates through an exotic striptease/self-suck/self-fuck routine for an audience of about 20 men. Some of these men masturbate, others merely watch (perhaps resting in between their own sexual interludes). The film captures an interesting performer-audience dynamic, as well as

---

*Few are still in operation. Back rooms in nightclubs and safe sex clubs (both of which usually provide ample supplies of condoms) have begun to take the place of bathhouses as gay male sexual playgrounds.

**For a fine anthropological text on the subject see Joseph Styles's "Outsider/ Insider: Researching Gay Baths" in *Urban Life*, July 1989.

an interesting dynamic among the patrons in general. Elsewhere in the film, these same men are seen engaging in sexual activity with one another. When they meet for the stage show, they are no longer sexual participants, but rather, voyeurs. Scott deftly captures the role mutability within the gay bathhouse.

Other gay films similar to *Turned On* in that they document a level of gay male lifestyle not often addressed through other means are Jack Deveau's *A Night at the Adonis* (1978, Hand in Hand) and Fred Halsted's *A Night at Halsted's* (1982, HIS Video). The Adonis, a now-relocated Manhattan gay male porn palace featuring first-run films and male strippers, is adequately documented in Deveau's film. I am unaware of any relevant writings on the space. Fred Halsted established a bar in Los Angeles "for leathermen and trendy porn performers to gather" (Rowberry 1990, p. 162), and then made a movie about it. *A Night at Halsted's* is just what the title says: a pornumentary on the exploits of the bar's patrons shot over the course of an evening. What is interesting in this film is the documenting of the architectural extremes to which some gay bars went in order to create and fulfill certain men's sexual fantasies: the bar's back lot was equipped with two or three empty 18-wheeler rigs, open and ready for truck stop fantasies.* This bar is another piece of gay male culture undocumented except in a porn film.

The New York piers, notorious for gay male sexual liaisons, are now, like most bathhouses, only a memory in the gay male consciousness.** As a piece of historic architecture, the piers are well documented. As an important gay cultural social and sexual space, they are not. Steve Scott's film *Non-Stop* (1984, Bijou Video) incorporates one scene shot in the piers. This scene is a great record of both the architecture of the piers and the effects the architecture had on the cruising habits of the men that frequented them. Sprawling and labyrinthine, the piers encouraged sexual cat-and-mouse pursuits. Scott's film captures this practice well, devoting a substantial amount of film time to the cruise/chase of two men. The actual

---

*Similar to the semi trailer in New York City's now defunct Man's Country bathhouse.

**Though, as of the summer of 1992, a newly abandoned pier in the same district has been colonized.

sexual consummation is, as a subject of study, unspectacular compared to the chase. The expansiveness of the pier and the sexual anxieties and expectancies it must have produced are what the film expertly portrays. There are no written texts I know of which adequately recreate this gay male experience indigenous to New York. *Non-Stop* is an excellent documentation of the piers' place in contemporary gay male history.

Boys in the Sand (1972, TMX Video) is of minor historical interest as a document of gay male culture; it is more notable as a document of gay male sexual practices. This film, starring Casey Donovan, follows the sexual exploits of vacationers at The Pines on Fire Island. Should The Pines succumb to an all-out heterosexualizing, *Boys in the Sand* will stand as a major historical text. Other, more contemporary porn videos document the existence of all-gay male vacation resorts. Unfortunately, they mostly document that existence in the abstract; specific resorts are rarely named. Falcon Studios' *Revenge: More Than I Can Take* (1990) is set at a gay resort hotel, probably in Palm Springs. It portrays the sexual relations between staff and guests, and documents the relaxed atmosphere of such retreats. Pool-side, the men admire one another, openly discuss their sexual preferences, and so forth. Here is a secluded and private environment, free from the oppression of compulsory heterosexuality.

Other examples of videos celebrating the all-gay resort (or the like) are Ron Pearson's *Sighs* (1985, Bijou Video), about the goings-on at a gay health club, and Falcon Studios' *The Other Side of Aspen I* and *II* (1980, 1985) about a gay ski lodge. These videos, and others like them, are important documents not only of the all-gay environment, real or invented, but of the gay male psyche which so desperately envisions such spaces where they can be free from the social oppressions encountered daily. The invention of the pornutopia is a vital aspect of the gay male experience. In our marginalization, we have created these bars, clubs, and sexual spaces as sanctuaries. If we must be marginalized, let us at least create enjoyable spaces on the fringe–whether in imaginary representations (such as *The Other Side of Aspen II*) or in reality, like the bathhouses.

But with the spread of AIDS, the social order has deemed it necessary to close down many of these sanctuaries. Bathhouses and sex clubs are not so abundant as they once were. Many spaces that were distinctly gay men's, and once untouched by the heterosexual order, are now gone, "for our own good." The margins are being narrowed. It is difficult for new forms of sexual asylum to arise in the face of a leviathan health issue such as AIDS.* It is necessary to retain the images and memories of these now extinct gay spaces, and continually document the extant examples, so we can progressively learn from our mistakes and our defeats, and create new and stronger replacements, and so that future generations of gay men can see where we have been, and what a pleasure it was to be there.

Recording the Present

A recent development in the porn industry, more in the straight market than in the gay, is the popularity of commercially marketed amateur home porn videos. The best gay male example of this phenomenon is *Al Parker's Sexiest Home Videos* (1991, Surge). These amateur sequences range, aesthetically and erotically, from hot to inane. The camera work is often clumsy or uninventive, the lighting is poor, but the performances are sometimes remarkable. After all, these are exhibitionists who, without benefit of professional video production services, have nonetheless gone out of their way to document their sexual skills for the viewers' voyeuristic pleasure. These amateur porn videos are visual autobiographies of the sexual tastes and desires of a usually private sector of gay men. And, unlike many autobiographies, there is no monetary gain for the participants. By giving a little piece of their sex lives to their viewing audience, these men are marking their place in the visual history of the private lives of contemporary gay men.

Another type of gay porn video fits into this category of gay representation but is, at the same time, a meta-commentary on gay porn culture. These videos are generalized and, to an extent, fictionalized accounts of the making of gay male pornography. Six exceptional examples are *The Rise* (1990, Catalina), *New Love* (1990,

---

*Even the new back rooms and sex clubs mentioned earlier often come under police and health department attacks.

Panther Productions), *The Next Valentino* (1988, Horizon Video), *Sex, Lies, and Video Cassettes* (1989, Sierra Pacific), *Better Than Ever* (1989, Surge Studios), and *On the Rocks* (1991, Stryker Productions). Each offers a selective rendering of the gay male porn industry. Problems surrounding the filmic machinations of porn sex are eliminated from these representations. Instead, what the viewer sees is yet another type of pornutopia: a film set where man-to-man sex happens without a hitch, and where success and stardom are guaranteed for the actors portrayed.

Often, porn success is played against "legitimate" film success. *The Next Valentino* is about a newcomer, played by Kevin Glover, to the gay porn world. This rookie turns out to be so good at what he does, a "natural" as it were, that the porn industry directors and producers assure him success in the legitimate world of Hollywood; he is, in their opinions, the next Rudolph Valentino. In contrast is *Sex, Lies, and Video Cassettes*, which serves to legitimate gay porn by contrasting its production ethics to the lack thereof in the Hollywood movie industry. Joey Stefano, a "legitimate" actor, cannot get that big Hollywood break which he so deserves because he refuses to sleep with the executives, moguls, and casting-couch producers, whereas Jared Young, a gay porn actor, lives a much happier life by working in the porn industry. There, the producers respect him; there is no professional hanky-panky. In the end, thanks to his porn popularity, Young snags a "legitimate" film audition and lands the role, while Stefano contemplates a career change to blue movies.

These videos set up a fantastic relation between two different sectors of the film industry. They both use the "legitimacy" of Hollywood, in two highly divergent ways, to legitimate the trade to which they belong. Porn is either a good, solid stepping-stone to Hollywood, or is seen, in comparison to unethical Hollywood, as a preferable area in which to work. *Sex, Lies, and Video Cassettes* leaves open the question of how Stefano and Young will do in each other's former industries. The viewer feels that Young, having received the educational benefits of working in the porn business, will fare much better in Hollywood than Stefano, but that Stefano should soon follow in Young's footsteps.

By producing videos of this sort, the gay male porn industry is attempting to combat the social stigmatization of its work. It is an idealist practice, one which must be studied with some discretion. What are these videos documenting, if anything? Obviously not the real working and set conditions in the porn industry, nor the realities of career choices and employment difficulties. Rather, such videos document a state of mind current among many sex workers (prostitutes, porn stars, and others involved in the "selling" of sex): a sense of pride in their work. Groups such as Prostitutes of New York (PONY), Call Off Your Old Tired Ethics (COYOTE), and the publishers of *Whorezine* are forerunners of moves to legalize and legitimate the sex industry. These movements sometimes work with, sometimes against, the gay and feminist movements (most notable here is the antagonism between WAP and PONY). Videos such as *The Next Valentino* capture the surge of pride within the sex work industry. These videos do not document the politics of this pride, but rather, treat it as a given. They create a utopian world in which porn is as legitimate a career as law or medicine. Perhaps these films are not idealizing the present so much as envisioning the future—putting forth porn industry ideals, future states and conditions for which to strive; porn videos as utopian manifestoes.

One last video which merits discussion within this structure of gay porn as recorder of the present is the 1992 Mustang release *Sex Shooters II*. It opens with actor Ted Matthews telling an acquaintance about how he broke up a fag-bashing incident the previous week, then took the young victim to his home to clean him up. The next scene is a flashback. Matthews leads the young, blond victim into his bathroom. The guy's face is bruised and blood-caked. They talk tentatively of the cowardice of the two bashers while getting into the shower. Every few seconds they delicately kiss. In between kisses, Matthews makes remarks like: "It looks like they really roughed you up." Eventually Matthews takes a sponge and begins to very gently wash the blood away from the young man's face. The scene is very slow and sensuous, but also difficult to watch, not only because of the controversial subject matter which forms the basis of the scene's narrative, but because the blond guy occasionally flinches away from the sponge, looking like a frightened and untrusting animal, and lending the scene an extra level of realism. When the blood is washed away, Matthews romantically and tenderly kisses the blond's face. Then they make love.

Fag-bashing, for any out-of-the-closet gay man or lesbian, is a constant threat. Fag-bashing scenarios are not the sort of things that are often represented in our sexual fantasies–the erotic potential of the Florence Nightingale syndrome notwithstanding. *Sex Shooters II* addresses the issue of fag-bashing, but leaves much unsaid. On the one hand, the video is a rare instance of gay porn dealing with a subject that threatens gay men on the basis of their sexuality. Gay pornography generally posits that gay sex is good; *Sex Shooters II* delivers the scary truth that some people disagree–sometimes violently–with this position.

On the other hand, this video offers no venting of the outrage, the anger, and the hurt which accompany such incidents. The crime and its ramifications are given no political context. Here, the sexual caresses of the young man's Good Samaritan are enough to alleviate his pain. His anger, personal or political, never surfaces, and is never processed. Surely he must feel *some* anger. By disallowing this victimized character any emotional or political outlet for his pain, by offering sex as the only necessary antidote for this hurt, the producers of this video fall far short of their erotic intent. The nature of this scene is scary. The incident which generates the erotic interlude is too powerful; its emotional consequences for the viewer are not so easily subsumed by the ensuing gentle love-making. It is difficult to get turned on by the blood of a fag-bashing victim. Kisses do not wash away the deeper scars.

So, although *Sex Shooters II* documents a fearful aspect of the gay communities' current existence, it fails to put it into the political context necessary for physical and mental healing. The cum shot does not deliver the justice demanded by the viewer's riled mind. The popular memory of the gay culture is indeed expanded by the content of this video. But the selectivity of the producers' memory leaves the popular memory incomplete, and the viewer's erotic satisfaction guilt-ridden and disturbed, if not cancelled out altogether.

Pornlore

The video *On the Rocks* directly addresses something which I will term "pornlore." In the gay male community, pornlore consists of rumors, stories, truths, and anecdotes surrounding the icons and images of the industry. Many stars acquire large reputations. Jeff

Stryker, for instance, has a notorious reputation for being straight–a reputation he capitalizes on. In a recent *Interview* interview, Stryker responds to the question of whether he has a boyfriend by saying "I have a partner" (1990, p. 135). Questioned further as to why he does not specify sex, Stryker says:

> Because it'll leave something to the imagination. And as far as my image in adult films goes, I try not to categorize myself as straight or gay, because I don't want to limit myself to one particular market. I don't like to stereotype any person because of race, creed, color, religion, or anything. (Ibid.)

Stryker constructs a sexually ambiguous persona for himself. After his first few films, most gay men, although wishing him to be gay, believed otherwise. In his early films, Stryker is always the topman; he never sucks or gets fucked, or kisses another guy (except for, perhaps, a quick and tongueless peck, like with Steve Hammond in *Stryker Force* [1987, Huge Video]). Most gay men know of Stryker's topman status–his sexual exploits on screen most likely reflect his everyday preferences as well. He is, rumoredly, "gay for pay," although there is no concrete substantiation. This is one example of pornlore.

Then came the movie *Powerfull II* (1989, Stryker Productions). In this film, directed by Stryker himself, this pornlore was proven inaccurate. After its release, everyone dubbed it "the movie in which Jeff Stryker sucks cock." And he does, although not very heartily. Thus the pornlore of "Stryker as topman only" was discredited. But the actual concept of "pornlore" itself was not addressed directly, until the release of *On the Rocks*. In this video Stryker plays himself. He has a scene in a private gym with costars Matt Gunther and Joey Stefano. Gunther plays a porn star hopeful, asking trade tips of Stefano. Stryker enters and is immediately recognized as the mega-porn star that he is. While assisting Gunther on the bench press, Stryker receives a blow job from him. During this, Stefano approaches Stryker and asks, "Why do you never kiss in your videos?" This is an instance of pornlore surfacing in and being directly addressed by porn itself. Stryker responds by pulling Stefano in close to him, and initiating a long wet French kiss (but he still does not suck or get fucked). Whether Stryker is evidencing his true sexual desires or his marketing genius is unimportant here. The acknowledgement by porn of porn's own mythological presence within gay culture is an interesting instance of reflexivity. *On the Rocks* shows Stryker showing Stefano that pornlore, first of all, exists and, second, may often be inaccurate. The producers of *On the Rocks* have also documented the "voice" of their viewers, something not often witnessed in porn videos. This filmic trope points to future possibilities for porn video's interactive relationship with its audience. If the need for the construction of a pornlore can be acknowledged by video producers, then possibly many other community desires (sexual, cultural, or political) might also be so intimately addressed.

All of the films discussed in this chapter actively fulfill a vital premise put forth by the Popular Memory Group that "the recreation of popular struggles shows us that despite retreats and defeats, 'the people,' 'the working class,' or the female sex [and gay communities] *do* 'make history' even under conditions of oppression or exploitation" (1982, p. 212). Gay porn recreates the struggles of history (Native American genocide, the Vietnam War, etc.), as well as the struggles of the self (sexual negotiation within homosocial spheres, self-legitimation of porn as a career, and so forth). The obvious next step in the representation of popular struggles to be addressed by the industry are the even more personalized struggle of coming out, and the greater social struggles of gay rights and AIDS activism.

Chapter IV

One Step Forward, Two Steps Back

In the 1985 *Jump Cut* article "Men's Pornography: Gay vs. Straight," author Tom Waugh suggests that "gay porn functions as potential regressive force, valorizing sexism, looks-ism, sizeism, racism, ageism, and so on, as well as violent behaviors" (1985, p. 33). Waugh rightly contends that gay male porn does, to an extent, valorize these regressive conditions of racism and ageism. Violence, however, is a different matter altogether. Applicably, The Popular Memory Group puts forth that

> the study of popular memory . . . is a necessarily relational study. It has to take in the dominant historical representations in the public field as well as attempts to amplify or generalize subordinated or private experiences. Like all struggles it must needs have two sides. Private memories cannot, in concrete studies, be readily unscrambled from the effects of dominant historical discourses. It is often these that supply the very terms by which a private history is thought through. Memories of the past are, like all common-sense forms, strangely composite constructions, resembling a kind of geology, the selective sedimentation of past traces. (1982, p. 211)

In other words, given the current (and past) state of American society, it is logical that gay male pornographic representations, regardless of how liberal or radical they may appear, accommodate (perhaps unconsciously) the racist and ageist norms that occupy the American psyche. Many gay male videos are "thematically" devoted to all-black, all-Latin, and to a much lesser degree, all-Asian casts, older "daddy" types, or sadomasochism (which is often, but without basis, regarded by nonpractitioners as "violent"). *The Adam*

Film World 1991 Directory: Gay Adult Video* lists in its "theme" breakdown: 28 all-black cast videos, 29 videos under the heading "Latinos," 18 "interracial sex" videos, 18 "leather/SM" videos, no heading for Asian videos, and no heading for older men or "daddies." (In the latter theme, only three relatively recent films even come to mind: *40 Plus* [1987, Live Video, Inc.] by Scott Morgan, *Chip Off the Old Block* [1985, HIS Video] by Jim West, and *Working Stiffs* [1990, Altomar/Adam & Co.] by Thor Johnson. Of the latter, John Rowberry in *The Adam Film World* guide writes: "Director Thor Johnson fails to glamourize unattractive (but sincere) guys in this hodgepodge of labor-related situations" [1990, p. 171]. No mention is made of their age.)

It is important to look at these genres of gay video as examples of how the dominant social order influences and shapes our self-representations. The gay communities are obviously not immune to racism, ageism, and violence. These conditions are too deeply imbedded in the white male heritage to be easily eradicated. That out of over 1,000 videos listed in the directory, only 57 feature racial minorities is a depressing indicator of how easily gay white men marginalize nonwhites. The same applies to the "forty-plus" crowd, and even the "thirtysomething" group, for that matter.

BACKWARD STEP #1: RACISM

No video rental demographics are available, but from experiences with video retailers in New York, Chicago, Detroit, and Los Angeles, I presume that the majority of renters (and purchasers) are white males. Judging from the titles of some of the "race" videos, *Black Shafts, Black Sweat, Colored Boys, Ebony Eagles, Boys of El Barrio, Homeboy Workout, Horse Hung Hispanics, Raunchy Ricans, Oriental Dick,* and *My Thai Guy,* it seems safe to assume that most of these films are marketed toward white male viewers. Granted, they may often be line-produced and directed by men of color, but the pejorative nature of most of the titles resonates with the injustice of the white erotic subordination of ethnic minorities. It is difficult to believe that a Puerto Rican director aiming a video at a

---

*Subsequent editions do not include video breakdowns according to theme.

Puerto Rican market would title his venture *Raunchy Ricans*. True, it is often the case that oppressed minority groups appropriate the pejorative and racist slang used against them as a political tool–a sort of verbal self-mortification: doing the damage before the oppressor can, thereby thwarting their hatred. Thus, gay men often refer to themselves and others among their ranks, as "fags," "queers," and the like. This occurs among many minorities, racial, religious, or sexual. But such appropriations are never utilized by the white segment of the gay porn industry. There are no films with titles like *Wimpy White Boys* or even *Filthy Faggots*. Consequently it is likely that films such as *Colored Boys* and *Raunchy Ricans* implicitly practice racist methodologies, regardless of who produces or directs them. One is most apt to find, behind these all-black, all-Latin, and all-Asian videos, white capital pulling the strings and naming the names.

In a recent panel discussion on gay pornography, black actor Cord Colby addressed the issue of ethno-specific videos (1991). Colby resolutely refuses to participate in such films, stating that the companies that produce them will not hire him for projects that do not have all-black casts. To date, he has appeared only in racially integrated videos which bear no "interracial" euphemisms in their titles. Colby, however, has still encountered incidents of racism within these integrated productions. Many white porn stars (even some with which Colby has had outside relations) refuse to perform with him on camera, claiming that to do so would be a "bad career move." The potential racism of the viewing audience here perpetuates racist practices within the industry for the purpose of career longetivity.

It is also possible to regard the derogatory titles of these videos as racist disclaimers of sorts. These titles act more as warning labels than sensual enticement. *Black Attack* and *Horse Hung Hispanics* denote racial and sexual subjugation for those who want it, and "stay away" for those who need to maintain segregational practices in their sexual fantasies. In either case, it is the ethnic minority which is stigmatized, treated as variant, marginalized by the already marginal. Of the 27 all-black cast videos listed in *The Adam Film World* guide, 17 incorporate the word "black," or a euphemistic variation, into their titles. Of the 29 Latin films, 19 have racially explicative titles. And of the 18 interracial videos, eight titles "warn" of their racial content. Most all-Asian films follow this same pattern, though no actual numbers are readily available.

In the majority of porn films the absence of men of color is quite glaring, sometimes crassly so, as in the case of *1230 Melrose Place* (1992, Catalina). This particular video follows the exploits of a group of white male apartment building tenants forced by police curfew to cancel their plans for a night out during the 1992 L.A. race riots. Not only are black men excluded from the storyline's sex scenes, it is implied that they are the cause of the young white men's disappointments and inconveniences. The white men prove they can still have a good time without, and despite, men of color. This lame and socially indifferent excuse for a plotline is a particularly embarrassing episode in the current trend of gay pornography. It is a blatant rejection of racial difference and an unsympathetic and unconstructive treatment of important social issues.

Representational ideologies vary greatly vis-à-vis the different subjugated "races" within these videos. The treatment of African-American and Latino men, for example, celebrates their mytho-erotic stature of being super-endowed. This particular instance of sexual-racial stereotyping falsely empowers these men of color with a "threatening hypersexuality" (Fung 1991, p. 146). This empowerment, however, is undermined by the "hyper" quality of the sexual stigma, for it, in a sense, dehumanizes these "super-endowed" races: "the Negro is eclipsed. He is turned into a penis. He *is* a penis" (Frantz Fanon quoted in Fung 1991, p. 148).

The case of the Asian man is just the opposite. Sexual-racial discourse often constructs the Asian man as harmless and sexless. Whereas there is an abundance of all-black and all-Latin gay porn videos, very few all-Asian videos are on the market. In fact, very few videos incorporating even one Asian actor exist. Richard Fung, in his illuminating essay on the topic, "Looking For My Penis: The Eroticized Asian in Gay Video Porn," analyzes the desexualizing treatment undergone by Asian actors in the industry. Their industry names are often trite racist puns (for example, Sum Yung Mahn, who appears in *Below the Belt* [1986, Bijou Video] and *International Skin* [1985, N'wayvo Richhe]). More often than not Asians assume the passive sexual position in these videos, an exception being the 1986 International Wavelength release *Studio X*, promoted with the claim that "Sum Yung Mahn makes history as the first Asian who fucks a non-Asian" (quoted in Fung 1991, p. 153.) Often they are the subjects of colonialistic fantasies (such as the sexually subservient houseboy in *Asian Knights* [1985, Le Salon], or the young samurai warrior sexually vanquished by a white man in *Below the Belt*).

Race and racism are problematic issues in the eroto-political arena of gay male video pornography. In the above examples, porn as popular memory is undermined by the influences and permeations of the dominant memory's racist discourse. Such videos are regressive instances in the forward movement of gay and civil rights. Although gay porn may radically rewrite much of history, it unfortunately has not radically positivized the situations of gay men of color in this country.

BACKWARD STEP #2: AGEISM

Scott Morgan's *40 Plus* was advertised through mail-order brochures thus:

> If you want to see REAL MEN tangling in the kind of action that only gutsy know-how can provide, then get these ADULTS on your screen as fast as you can. There's a rugged fisting scene, there's sweet, hot fucking with a touch of romance, there's [sic] businessMEN who strip from suits to leather for some serious fucking and dildo play. And there's a splash of water sports that'll make you think you're going to get wet. Nearly an hour of mature sex you'll never forget.

The case of older men in gay male video pornography poses a confounding problem. On the one hand, it is obvious that most gay porn videos involve young, handsome boys and men–unfortunate looks-ism practiced to satisfy consumer demand for idealized sexual fantasy. (Very few porn actors work past their mid-20s.) On the other hand, one may assume that a large amount of porn is viewed by older men who want to see younger men (again, no demographics are available to justify this statement; it is an experiential hypothesis). Of course, this assumption stems from the ageist inclinations this society has regarding sexual relationships. A large separation in age between partners is considered "unnatural." Typically, youth is equated with beauty, age with wisdom. And unfortunately, wisdom is not easily visually eroticized, especially in pornography, in which the performers are not necessarily "actors." Age and maturity, therefore, take an unwarranted back seat in the realm of visual erotics.

But this is not always the case in real life. Many young men enjoy satisfying relationships with older men. In practice, maturity, wisdom, and experience may be very attractive to younger men. Conversely, the younger man's "greenness," innocence, and so forth may be attractive to the older partner. Pornography has trouble depicting this emotional bond. There are, however, a few well-intentioned attempts, such as *Chip Off the Old Block* (HIS Video, 1985), in which two young guys on a camping trip with their fathers relate father/son sex stories, then proceed to have a four-way with their own dads.

Other videos depict the attraction more mature men have for one another. As mentioned earlier, *Working Stiffs* and *40 Plus* are two of the better recent examples. During the 1970s there was a much greater proliferation of older men in porn videos: Richard Locke and Fred Halsted were both well into their mid-30s at the peaks of their careers. Films like *El Paso Wrecking Corp.*, *Kansas City Trucking Co.*, *L.A. Tool & Die*, and *Heat Stroke* all feature older men in starring roles. Younger, more experientially naive guys are never paired together in these videos. If featured at all, it is as novitiate playthings for the more mature men. The decline in number of representations of the mature male in gay pornography coincides with the 1982 advent of the ego-dystonic homo-video discussed earlier. Even though the industry has seemingly recovered from this period of self-loathing, the incorporation of older men into the hardcore action has never fully regained the momentum it picked up in the 1970s. Older men do, however, dominate the subgenre of s/m porn videos. In a sadomasochistic relationship, age necessarily presupposes sexual skill and expertise, especially in the topman role. The successful enactment of s/m practices depends upon men deftly skilled in both top and bottom positions. Such skill is achieved only through time and practice, often spanning many years for the topman.

Unfortunate as this recent dearth of mature men in the genre may be, the few videos which do address the age issue demonstrate a very real respect for these men. It is possible that the current lack of non-s/m porn videos with this subject matter points equally to ageism and to the representational difficulties of the complex emotional workings of such relationships.

* * *

I return here to a quote by the Popular Memory Group cited earlier. "These [manifestations of popular memory] may have a negative force, warning, for instance, against returns to past disasters" (1982, p. 212). This is how one must regard these ageist and racist videos: as current examples of the inequities of the dominant social order trickling down into the minorities it oppresses. That these videos exist serves to warn the gay communities that they are not immune to the deeply imbedded prejudices this country practices. We must study these films as negative manifestations of our popular memory, insidiously influenced by the many bigots in this society. Perhaps by expressing these prejudices in a visual medium, by putting them before our eyes, we can begin to see our own shortcomings and hypocrisies. And perhaps then we can begin to eradicate them from our lives. As liberationists, the gay communities must not practice an erotics of segregation or subjugation. Intergenerational and racially integrative sexual relations should be representational givens, not treated as something kinky and deviant.

ONE STEP FORWARD: SADOMASOCHISM

When Tom Waugh writes of "violent behaviors" it is not exactly clear what he means. It is doubtful that he is referring to such instances as the badly choreographed fist-fight in *El Paso Wrecking Corp.* or the pseudo-rape in *Men of the Midway* (1983, Le Salon) in which Chris Burns has to assist in his own rope binding. Perhaps Waugh is addressing the gender stereotypes of dominant/submissive and the power inequalities associated with them. Nowhere in gay culture does this power dichotomy come more into play than in the s/m subculture.

Contrary to majority opinion, s/m is, at least to its practitioners, not about violence. S/m is also not a glorification of rape, nonconsensual subjugation, or gendered power struggles. In order to better understand what it is about, it is necessary to discuss some of the theories of s/m put forth by its practitioners and community members. These same men produce the pornographic video representations of s/m which will subsequently be discussed.

One can categorize s/m practices into two divisions: physical pain, and emotional (or mental) pain. The infliction of physical pain is the most essential quality of s/m and therefore many theories about its purposes have been written. The notion of a "shift in consciousness" as promoted by the infliction of pain is central to most of these arguments. In his book *Urban Aboriginals*, Geoff Mains states that the s/m ritual of giving and receiving pain ". . . is accompanied by a significant shift in consciousness. The individual has come to accept association with a tribe, with the attitudes held by that tribe, and with the conflicts those attitudes can create in the ambient world" (1984, p. 24). The tribe of which Mains speaks is the gay male s/m community. This shift in consciousness can be manifested in any number of ways. Current thought puts biochemistry at the forefront of these arguments, positing that, upon receiving pain, the body and brain release endorphins and opioids which result in an altered state of consciousness, ranging anywhere from light trance to hysteria (Ibid., pp. 55-6). Although intriguing, there is not yet enough empirical scientific data to confirm this view.

Mains, summarily discussing the bonds which unite the leather tribe, goes on to say:

> As a sub-culture leather refracts the values of western society to create its own vision. It takes images of masculinity, the use and abuse of power, and the values of creativity, and it pits them against the perils of human arrogance and the realities of human limits. It creates from all of this an experience that is cathartic, ecstatic, and spiritual. (Ibid., pp. 20-1)

Here, the three words "cathartic," "ecstatic," and "spiritual" are very important because they arise in two other influential texts from the culture. In *The Leatherman's Handbook II*, Larry Townsend essentializes s/m into the sole element of catharsis: "Recently, we have found some students of social science recognizing SM practices as an enormous catharsis, the healthy venting of energies that might otherwise prove destructive. That is the answer if you really need one" (1983, p. 19). In this model, someone like Waugh's conception of violence is recodified into a practice meant to undermine the potential for violence itself.

Purusha (born Peter Larkin), in his books *The Divine Androgyne: Adventures in Cosmic Erotic Ecstasy* and *Androgyne Bodyconsciousness*, validates the practice of s/m (here primarily exemplified in body piercing and fistfucking) through a condensed montage of global spiritual philosophies, ranging from Gnostic mysticism to Buddhism to Tantric myths of the Kundalini serpent. Purusha grounds his theory of s/m in the complementary yin and yang energies of Buddhism. That is, in order to be psychosexually liberated from socially enforced repressions of sexuality, one must fully explore both erotic pleasure and its complement, erotic pain. For example, Purusha speaks of fistfucking as that "which produces the most intense orgasm and highest ecstatic level experienced so far by males; and all the components for an experience of ritual rebirth which culminates in great ecstasy" (1981, p. 33). Sadomasochism, as regarded by these three authors, is a religious experience of sorts, achieved via the body in sexual pain.

According to these writers, the infliction of emotional or mental pain works on the same principles as the infliction of physical pain. Submission, domination, and humiliation all work toward the goal of ego-transcendence. In the consensual acting out of society's highly gendered power struggles, s/m practitioners deconstruct these repressive stigmatizations in the safety of the "bedroom theater." According to Purusha, the androgyne (i.e., the gay male s/m practitioner), in accepting both his masculine and feminine qualities (more abstractly represented–that is, to Western thought–by the yin and the yang) in thought and practice, transcends the artificial constructs of power and gender enforced by the hegemonic social order (Ibid., p. 93).

In the construction of the gay male s/m body, then, the various inflictions of pain serve the purpose of mind expansion, shifting of consciousness, and spiritual transcendence of the body. The body is the channel through which one must pass in order to transcend its corporeality; pain is the tool with which to initiate this process. How these ideologies are represented in pornographic videos, however, is a separate question. For those uninitiated or uninterested in the practices of s/m, the portrayal on film of these acts might very well appear to be violent.

The extreme and potentially objectionable subject matter of s/m videos mostly relegates their accessibility to mail-order businesses. The content of these videos often includes genitorture, tit-torture, bondage, spanking, flagellation (with belts, whips, and canes), water sports (mostly external in the more recent videos, internal in the pre-AIDS-awareness videos), fetishes (leather, uniforms, and boots being among the most popular), and fistfucking. Piercing is rarely shown (exceptions being the videos *Unfriendly Persuasion* [n.d., Odyssey] and *Like Moths to a Flame* [1989, Marathon Films]), but men with preexisting piercings are often employed. Submission and dominance are always an element, while consensuality often is not. It is understood that the actors in the videos have consented to participate, and that, within the fantasy scenarios, playing at non-consensuality is often a key element, particularly in rape fantasies.

The subgenre of gay male s/m porn videos is as diversified as its encompassing parent genre. A common characteristic shared by most of them, though, is the contextual *mis en scène*. Most of these videos focus on s/m practitioners in their own particular milieu, usually an s/m dungeon. Very few present a fictional *mis en scène* which necessitates a willing suspension of disbelief in the viewer. One example of the latter is *Unfriendly Persuasion*. The video is set on a South American island penal colony. Here political prisoners are subjected to testicular flesh piercing, electrotorture, and urination, among other things. An epilogue to the video states that many of the experiences presented were influenced by real-life accounts of political prisoners supplied by Amnesty International–the difference being that in the video, the locale and the role-playing are all fantasy; the men are all getting a sexual kick out of their activities. The results of the torture are pleasurable, and nowhere near the extreme nature of actual political prisoner experiences. To cite Amnesty International case studies as an influence is an unnecessarily callous attempt to imbue a fantasy scenario with intimations of realism.

For this reason, most s/m porn videos avoid any attempt to make real a particular fantasy or fetish scenario. When two men role-play cop and robber, the latter subjected to (consensual) police brutality in the privacy of their own basement dungeon, a spectator witnesses only their individual sexual tastes and powerplay desires. Were a video to authentically represent the same situation, this time set in a precinct house, the depictions of s/m might become easily convoluted with actual images from instances of police brutality. That is, if s/m is "good" pain, and police brutality is "bad" pain, the erotic intent of the porn video may be undermined if the producers attempt to make "bad" pain visually pass for "good" pain. "Good" pain may resemble "bad" pain, however, so as to deconstruct society's gendered power struggles, as discussed earlier. So, whereas it is an erotic experience to view *Slave Workshop-Hamburg* (1990, Close Up), in which a young man answers a master's personal ad and is subsequently (and consensually) subjected to a severe kicking, it would not be erotic to watch a porn film that presents a similar scene in an intentionally realistic replication of the Rodney King videotape, regardless of the fact that the performances may be consensual. The constructive pain of s/m may often comment upon the other examples of destructive pain, but it does not attempt to *be* them. Therefore, s/m porn videos, for the most part, adhere to this same rule. When they do not, the viewers' sympathies may drift from the sexual to the social, and the pornography's erotic efficacy is often undone.

There are many video companies which produce s/m pornography in which the narrative context is that of a dungeonmaster's home playroom. Some of the better examples are: the *Dungeons of Europe* series, which includes *Pictures from the Black Dance* (1988, Marathon), *Like Moths to a Flame* (1988, Marathon), and *Men with No Name* (1989, Marathon), all credited to Roger Earl of *Born to Raise Hell* fame; the many bondage performance art videos from Zeus Studios in Los Angeles, in which muscle boys are bound and gagged with some of the most inventive and artistic restraining techniques imaginable, then roughed up by other muscle boys or anonymous hands; the videos of Christopher Rage, in which the "dungeon" is really the director's loft-size studio, where men gather to get kinky and raunchy for the camera; and the playful take on bondage and fetishism manifested in Bob Jones's videos, where men are bound then tickled, or subjected to prolonged foot worship.

Rage, who recently passed away, is one of the most experimental and radical of gay porn auteurs, and merits additional discussion. Through his many films, Rage documents a gay urban sexual sideshow. His videos are not for the squeamish. An incomplete listing of some of the acts presented in his works does not do justice to his catalogue but is nonetheless helpful to those unfamiliar with his *oeuvre*. This list includes: actor Scott Taylor sticking his tongue down his urethra; men drinking their own and others' urine from pilsner glasses; a man anally accommodating two fists at the same time; catheters; urine enemas; men squirting chocolate bars and Milk Duds out of their butts to be eaten by Rage himself; spanking; whipping; piss orgies; fist-fights; forced drag; and defecation. The subject matter alone is *outré* enough, but Rage's style of filmmaking itself outrageously pushes the limits of pornography. Episodes are chopped up and intercut with an almost Cageian/*I Ching* randomness, sometimes even subverting the natural flow of the sexual act. The audio tracks are otherworldly, incorporating what sound like extended mixes of warped minimalist records. And the films are not without a twisted sense of humor. In *Hidden Camera* (1989, Live Video), for instance, Rage intermittently appears throughout the film campily reciting Gloria Swanson's final line from *Sunset Boulevard* ("I'm ready for my close-up, Mr. DeMille") in a number of different, deconstructive tones and timbres.

Rage's bizarre take on sexploitation and his avant-garde directorial tendencies combine to make his videos an uncanny viewing experience. Although many others may participate in the acts Rage documents, his particular and peculiar presentational style bestows unique stature. Even after his death, his predecessors at Live Video, such as Jack Stone, are documenting the same type of sex act, but without Rage's signature filmic flair.

There are three videos which exemplify the extremes to which representations of humiliation in gay male s/m pornography can be taken. The first two are put out by the Los Angeles-based company Old Reliable. The videotapes produced by Old Reliable are often filmed in a low-rent West Hollywood apartment. The models, who participate in solo jack-off scenes or dual wrestling or boxing scenes, are often tough, unpolished, uneducated guys off the streets. Many of them are heterosexual. The fetishization of these straight men often results in the humiliation of the home viewer. For example, a model known only as Jeffrey appears in several different Old Reliable videotapes. Videotape Number 72 best exemplifies Jeffrey's humiliative tactics. Here, Jeffrey masturbates to climax; upon orgasm, he snarls at the camera, shakes his sperm-coated tool, and says "Queers, eat this!"

I, Rick, also by Old Reliable, is a video portrait of Rick, a straight hustler who likes to talk dirty and show off his body for all his "faggot" admirers. Rick bends over, exposing his butthole for the "homos" who like that sort of thing; but it's with a laughingly derisive "look, don't touch" attitude. Both models, hard up for cash, pose for the filmmaker, all the while insulting their audience, thereby keeping their heterosexual machismo intact. The viewer may, in a sense, be turning the humiliation around back at the model through the objectifying lens of the camera, but the contempt which leaves the mouths of these Old Reliable performers is really humiliation of an unconstructive nature. The videos are a literal valorization of the oppressor and the attendant gendered power struggles and inequalities. This is very different from the typical s/m ritualistic subversion of the same. The viewer of these two Old Reliable videos, among others, experiences not ego transcendence, but rather, ego abuse. Self-subjugation to the heterosexual male is a strange taste indeed.

In contrast to Old Reliable's video hetero-fetishism is a film from San Francisco's Palm Drive Video featuring a model named Butch. This film, in a very leather/camp tone, deconstructs the normative gender roles, making a straight male the object of sexual scorn. Butch is billed as "Aryan Biker Butch Stocky 5-8, 185# Ex-Con Fat Butt-Plug Cock! Prison Tattoos! Tear-Drop Tattoo from Left Eye! Ringed Tit Straight Daddy of 2 Sons Humiliated into Raping Himself." The best is yet to come, as the advertising brochure ensures:

VICIOUS S*H*O*C*K VIDEO EXPLOITS STRAIGHT DAD 3 DAYS OUT OF PRISON and hard-up for money. PSYCHO-LOGICAL BONDAGE! *Butch is not acting . . .* See a heavily tattooed man, with the smell of prison succulent on him, perform on command. See his SLAMMER EYES shift suspiciously. Day 3 after HARD TIME, Butch, tough as they come, is still conditioned to obey men in authority! WANNA PLAY "PRISON-GUARD-WITH-A-CAMERA" MAKING INMATE STRIP, *CHEW ON HIS SWEATY LONGJOHNS, LICK HIS JAIL-HOUSE 'PITS, AND BEAT HIS 7+ INCHES!* Jerk Yourself off to Butch's RESENTMENT! His RESISTANCE STEAMS FROM THE SCREEN! But he's a *HOMEBOY* wise to FORCED STRIP SEARCHES, choking on his ATTITUDE LIKE A PITBULL CORNERED AT OBEDIENCE SCHOOL . . . Butch has HORNY-FUCKER N-E-E-D-S, hungry to watch a straight video, knowing that to get a sight of pussy, he, in turn, has to be videoed . . . (PDV's female clients will applaud seeing REVENGE in a REDNECK STUD'S SEXUAL SUBMIS-SION.) . . . Butch hangs hard on to what's left of his pride while he exudes the RESENTMENT OF HUMILIATION at being turned into a SEX OBJECT SAME AS THE VIDEO PUSSY HE OBJECTIFIES . . . SEE A STRAIGHT MAN, UNFAMIL-IAR WITH THE SENSUALITY OF HIS OWN BODY, HU-MILIATED INTO RAPING HIMSELF! (See a 30-year-old DOG taught new tricks!) YOUR EYES and YOUR GUTS will react to the ONSCREEN DYNAMICS OF SEXUAL POWER AND RESENTFUL HUMILIATION. Nice people don't j/o to "politically incorrect" videos like this; but whoever said *YOU* were "NICE"? *Butch* ain't.

This video demonstrates the same fetishizing of straight men as the Old Reliable examples. Here, however, the gay objectifier, if you will, humiliates the typically objectifying heterosexual male, as opposed to the Old Reliable videos in which the gay would-be objectifier is humiliatingly counter-objectified by the on-screen image of the straight man. The political semiotics of these videos become confounding. Revenge, in the case of Butch, becomes sex, though not necessarily "politically correct." By some, the rants of Jeffrey and Rick are deemed erotic, and probably even less "politically correct." The erotic need for humiliation, whether given or received, is a complex psychosexual process not easily explainable. These videos do not explain. Their makers perceive these needs and attempt to document the experiential range of humiliation in which the viewer may wallow.

* * *

Accepting one's s/m proclivities has often been termed a "second coming out." To have visual proof that other men are engaged in the sort of activities about which one fantasizes is a necessary stage in the "leather career" (Levi Kamel 1983, p. 74). So the images of homemade dungeons and leather-bar backrooms, humiliating dirty-talkers and raunchy sex-play both reaffirm or introduce their existence for those who need to know, and, at the same time, document their existence and utilization, marking their place in the visible history of gay men. These videos, like others, are vital warehouses of gay male s/m cultural, psychical, historical, and practical knowledge. They are specific and highly charged examples of gay male popular memory which, once seen, are not quickly forgotten.

Chapter V

Ob/Scene

Much space has been devoted in this book to the discussion of gay male video pornography as a manifestation of the post-Stonewall gay male popular memory. However, not yet included in this discussion are many comments on the realities of the porn industry. The machinations of sexual fantasy are complex, and vary from director to director, as do working and set conditions. Also, it is necessary to note briefly some of the off-set conditions porn industry workers encounter. Some of the off-stage truths are not as noble as the interpretations herein of the final video products. The final representation does not often reflect the methods used to achieve it. However, this does not always constitute a criticism.

It is impossible to summarily discuss working and set conditions within the gay male porn industry. They differ greatly from film to film, director to director, and so forth. For general purposes, this chapter will briefly address a few directors and the ways in which they implement a porn film shoot.

THE TRADE

An interesting exposé on the making of a gay porn flick is the video *Madness & Method: The Making of "Knight Out with the Boys"* (1992, Abandon Pictures). This porn documentary chronicles the pre-production and behind-the-scenes events leading up to and occuring during the shooting of John Travis's *Knight Out with the Boys* (1992, Abandon Pictures). Included are interviews with Travis, several of the performers and orgy scene extras, and candid footage of the production crew at work and rest. The most interesting of the documentary's revelations is a short segment of footage covering the models' visual consent and release forms. Each model is videotaped while holding two pieces of identification next to his face (usually a driver's license and Social Security card). He then tells his stage name, date of birth, age, and that he has willingly consented to participate in the video production. Other instances of note are the reactions of the director, cast, and crew when the cameraman misses a cum shot, and a scene where four naked actors sit around moaning and talking dirty for wild sound to be dubbed into the film later in post-production. The actual film *Knight Out with the Boys* is a comparatively high-budget porn video (it was shot over a four-day period on a professional sound stage with numerous set changes) and is therefore not necessarily indicative of the general means of production within the rest of the industry.

Porn videos are produced on very low budgets. Actors earn any-where from $200 to $500* per scene, depending on their position (bottoms usually get paid more than tops), level of difficulty of sex act (a multi-dildoed fuck pays more than a glory hole blowjob), and number of people involved (a guy getting gang-banged makes more money than he would in a one-on-one situation; he also makes more than the gang-bangers). Porn actor Byron Rogers, however, claims that East Coast performers like himself are paid on a per scene basis, whereas California performers are paid per movie: "some of them get like $2,000 or $3,000 but usually it's for one or two movies" (quoted in Wall 1992, p. 20). The films usually star one or two actors in an average of two or three scenes, and feature an average of six other performers. The typical format of these videos consists of five scenes (sometimes four, but it rarely deviates from this structure, exceptions being renegade pornographers such as Christopher Rage, Palm Drive Video, and so forth). A big name star like Joey Stefano may make up to $3,000 for a few days' work. Lesser-known costars, appearing in only one scene, might make $200 or $500 a day, depending on the many positional variables. In terms of wages, the nature of the porn industry is somewhat exploitative, especially in

---

*It is important to keep in mind that, due to the constantly changing nature of the porn industry, the wages herein may be inexact, and are culled from many differing sources over the past few years. However, $200 per scene and $3,000 for two movies seem to be the extremes of the wage spectrum.

regard to the lesser-known performers, and especially in comparison with "legitimate" and unionized mainstream films. Unlike Hollywood actors, porn stars are not protected by unions. They receive no pension, welfare, or percentage of the film's returns. Although $1,000 per video may seem like a lot, in the long run it is still rather meager when compared to the long-term benefits offered by mainstream moviemaking. The majority of gay porn stars are not fortunate enough to become Jeff Strykers or Joey Stefanos. After five or six films (with a high-end estimated income of $3,000) their careers are over. For many, strip shows and prostitution supplement their video income. But to be fair, there are young men who are involved in the sex industry (whether videos, prostitution, or both) for pure sexual enjoyment, especially more recently with the advent of the various highly militant gay political movements. For others it is a career. And for some, it is a combination of the two. Danny Summers, for example, enjoys appearing in porn films, putting the money he earns from them toward his college education in pharmacology. While the gay porn industry may very well exploit many young men, there are others in the trade who revel in this professional alternative.

In producing these videos, most of the budget money is allocated for talent, marketing, crew, and film stock. For this reason, technical facilities (i.e., studio, edit bay, etc.) are often housed in the director's apartment, or an equally inexpensive location. In his autobiography, porn star Jack Wrangler describes director Jack Deveau's apartment/film facilities:

> Jack Deveau lived in a penthouse. So did his first cameraman, his assistant director, his stage manager, his still photographer, plus a few other technical personnel and an enormous number of friends . . . The apartment also doubled as a cutting room, an editing room, a screening room, a studio, a playroom, and a living room–practically self-contained. (Wrangler and Johnes, 1984, p. 125)

The year was 1977. Deveau was directing Wrangler in two features: *Hot House* and *Sex Magic* (both Hand in Hand). Both films were shot in Manhattan and both costarred Roger, an equally famous porn star of the period.

Under similar working conditions, director Joe Gage shot *Heatstroke* (1982, HIS Video). Gage, according to film extra David Young, employed his Manhattan loft apartment as a studio as well. In it, he shot two of the film's sex scenes, both orgies: the first, a fantasy circle jerk/orgy centered around star Casey Donovan, and the second, the film's orgy finale incorporating all the stars and supposedly set in a Wyoming bunkhouse (Young, 1991).

"Stealing" locations is another money-saving ploy. Filmmakers usually have to pay a substantial fee for the use of studios and locations (both public and private). "Stealing" locations means precisely that: filming in a space for which permission has not been granted by the owners or managers. Exterior scenes are often picked up this way. These days, the accessibility to and prevalence of video cameras in the public sector makes stealing locations relatively easy. People walking down the street with video cameras are quite common, and often go by unnoticed. In the period before video, men with movie cameras were much more conspicuous in these spaces, and therefore much more prone to questioning and discovery.

Another money-saving technique similar to "stealing" locations is asking for their donation. Gay-friendly porn supporters often donate their sites to these film-makers. Bar and nightclub owners, home-owners, and the like, are often quite open about providing spaces for gay male pornographers.

The budgets for these videos are remarkably low. Reportedly, the most expensive gay male porn film made to date is *Centurians of Rome*. This 1981 film was financed by a Brinks robbery,* and cost between $150,000 and $250,000 (Rowberry 1990; Rowberry 1986), although sources differ on this. This cost range (for a 90-minute feature film) is roughly equal to the cost of a low-budget 30-second television commercial. By paying the crew "under the table" in cash, the producers of gay porn videos sidestep the film unions and their mandatory minimum wages, pension funds, as well as job title duties and regulations. The actors are often booked through model/escort agencies. The agencies set the prices, receive the money, and subsequently pay the actors, retaining for themselves a percentage of the fee. Some of the bigger stars, like Jeff

---

*As the insurer of Brinks, Lloyds of London co-owns this film.

Stryker, have personal managers or manage themselves, and also retain more "image" control. Some stars are even under exclusive contract with certain studios.

* * *

The creation of a marketable erotic image is very important in the gay porn industry. Porn theorist Susie Bright refers to this image as the "Pornographic Man." In a November, 1990 lecture entitled "How to Read a Dirty Movie" Bright suggests that the true "Pornographic Man" embodies two qualities: first, that he exercise pornographic male competence (he gets it up, keeps it going, gets it off), and second, that he never, in gay porn especially, manifest qualities of feminization. In relation to heterosexual porn, Bright precedes "never" with "almost" (1990). There are, however, three gay videos which contradict Bright's premise: *Bat Dude* (1989, In Hand), *The Master of the Discipline* (1984, London Enterprises), and *Outrage* (1984, Live Video). These films feature men in female drag incorporated into the sexual acts. Many gay porn films feature drag queens in roles intended for "comic relief." The above videos use drag, however, as a sexual gimmick: the men in drag are top-men, which, if viewed in light of gender/power ideologies, suggests it is necessary for these men to retain a level of masculinity (via sex position) and not give over completely to this feminization, this removal of power.

Bat Dude, The Master of the Discipline, and *Outrage* are oddities of the genre.* The masculine image, or hyper-male image, as I prefer to term it, is essential to the success of gay male porn. Jeff Stryker is one of the most successful and well-promoted images of the "Pornographic Man." Stryker is a carefully constructed erotic persona: the brainchild of gay porn directors Matt Sterling and John Travis. In an interview with the two directors in *The Advocate,* Sterling says of their construction of Stryker:

---

*Recently, transgenderist (i.e., chicks-with-dicks, for the most part) videos have become quite popular. Also of note is Chi Chi LaRue's *Steel Garters* (1992, Catalina), the bisexual, cross-dressing fantasy video, in which women dress like men, men dress like women, and all gender and sexual preference borders are made very hazy.

We changed his image: He came [to Los Angeles] with a completely outdated hairdo and an outdated way of dressing. We showed him how to dress differently and how to comb his hair, and we had his teeth fixed. And in addition to that, we decided to create an image. My idea of creating an image was kind of a rebel–because when I look at him I see a little bit of a young Elvis Presley and a young Marlon Brando. So we went for the motorcycle image. (1989, p. 29)

The directors' up-front investment has paid off. Stryker has since gone solo, forming his own production company, which manufactures not only videos, but sex toys, magazines, and other Stryker paraphernalia (like playing cards) as well. Many other actors have attempted to follow in Stryker's wake.

Whereas Stryker's producers reinvented the topman image, Joey Stefano has reinvented the image of the bottom. He presents himself as a handsome, Italian, tattooed tough who loves to get fucked. The success of his image lies in his carefully constructed dichotomy of appearance and practice: he appears to be a topman, but practices the bottom position. Stefano is well-received by his audience. On a 1990 visit to New York he garnered favorable press in *Outweek* and Michael Musto's column in *The Village Voice*. His April 29 autograph-signing appearance at Mars, a West Side nightclub, was met with enthusiasm as hundreds of young men lined up for a chance to meet the "superstar." Many other actors with similar "superstar" potential, such as Rex Chandler, Lex Baldwin, and Ryan Idol, have since followed Stryker and Stefano's public relations examples.

TRICKS OF THE TRADE

In the machinations of the porn industry, image-making is the first and most essential step of the filmmaking process. Actors with marketable hyper-male images comprise a talent pool from which directors choose. The makers usually have a working title in mind, as well as an ideal cast. Once the cast has been selected, the video box cover is made. Then, with often less than 24 hours of shoot time, the video is produced. On the set, making the sex happen can often be a difficult procedure. Many tricks and gimmicks are employed to combat the problems of failed erections, orgasms not caught on film, and disinterest among costars.

Porn director Al Parker relied on nothing more than hope when filming two guys in the midst of sex. He used information he received from his actors during pre-shoot interviews in determining how to pair them together. Parker attempted to keep the men separated before filming, as he was trying to capture that erotic spark of spontaneity when two men meet; he merely "hope[d] that it clicked," (1990). To Parker, spontaneity is what makes a scene "hot." If that exists, everything after should easily fall into place. When available, however, he used real-life lovers in scenes, in order to sidestep these difficulties.

Other directors do not put such trust in providence. Porn extra David Young remembers director Joe Gage's ingenuity in constructing erotics. Gage, wanting to film a circle jerk/orgy around star Casey Donovan in his film *Heatstroke*, knew that, working within a limited budget, it would be difficult to afford enough men able to get it up on camera. In 1982, when the film was made, Gage (like Young) was an active member of the New York Jacks, a Manhattan men's jack-off club. Gage recruited on a volunteer basis about 20 of the club's members for this scene. He was fully aware that this close-knit group of men, well-acquainted with masturbating with and in front of each other, would be fully capable of fulfilling his directorial decisions (Young, 1991). He was right, and this scene is a veritable bonanza of masturbatory orgasms. Compared to many other similar orgy scenes, Gage's fares much better. Gage sidestepped potential ego disruptions among "stars" by employing a volunteer group of actors who remain faceless and egoless throughout the scene, and were able to perform on cue as well.

John Travis, as seen in the documentary *Madness & Method*, tends to coach his stars through every sexual move, and at the same time direct his cameramen and lighting assistants where to focus their attention. Travis then dubs in wild sound tracks in post-production to compensate for the presence of his voice on the consequently unusable synchronized sound tracks.

There are other ingenuities involved in making sex happen on camera. In the case of failed erections, there are two ways to solve the problem. The first method employs a fluffer. This is an off-camera person hired to keep the star erect by any means necessary (which, more often than not, is a blow job or a hand job)–the problem here, of course, being that, if the actor could not get it up with his scene partner, he probably will fail with the fluffer as well. Fluffers, then, are usually employed before the shooting of the scene begins. They help the stars relax and "get ready." Often times, filming is suspended while the star retires to a private room to get himself erect, returning to the set when this is accomplished.

The second possible solution to a failed erection is a double. The double is a guy with a similar-looking dick to that of the star, who stands in for the star when the star loses his erection. Nineteen ninety newcomer Ryan Idol, in a *Frontiers* interview, confirms the rumor that ever-hard porn star David Ashfield dick-doubled for him in Idol's debut film *Idol Eyes* (1990, Sterling Express):

> It was my first film, and being nervous on top of everything else, it was easier for me to do it that way. It happens on first films. It was really new for me–not the sex, but doing it on film in front of eight people. I never had anybody tell me how to have sex before. My next film (with Dcota) will be the real thing. (1991, p. 42)

There are also butt-doubles in the industry. If an actor cannot or refuses to be anally penetrated, a butt-double is employed to take his place. Later takes can be shot, choreographed so it appears that the star is actually being fucked. In close-ups, dick-doubles and butt-doubles are usually unrecognizable. The close-up, then, can be regarded not as a necessarily subjugating tactic of objectification, but rather as a filmic necessity employed to successfully present and maintain the fantasy commingling of two men which might otherwise be marred by physical and emotional limitations. The film *Screwing Screw Ups* (1991, In Hand) is a compilation of comic gay porn video mishaps and out-takes indicative of the problems encountered on set; a blue movie "Bloopers," as it were. And the documentary *Madness & Method* captures the many times director John Travis calls "cut" during a sex scene, making it nearly impossible for the actors to maintain their erections.

Orgasms are often missed by the cameramen (again, see *Madness & Method*). For this reason, multiple cum shots are filmed, often at the expense of film continuity. Many times one sees in a porn film two men approaching orgasm. One shoots, say, on his own chest. There is a cut to the next shot, in which the viewer sees the second guy ejaculate, also onto the chest of the first guy. Only now, the first guy's chest no longer has any cum on it. Chances are good that the two guys did not climax simultaneously, as the film-makers would have one believe. Also, many porn stars refrain from having an orgasm for days before a shoot, so that their on-screen climax is much more dramatic and copious, and therefore more easily captured by the camera. And in the case of cut-away shots (i.e., to show cum dripping down someone's face) there are many alternatives to the real thing: "Cornhusker's lotion, Tame, and Italian Balm" (Pat Rocco quoted in Siebenand 1975, p. 72).

Films not employing synch-sound have other recourses for not missing the actors' orgasms. David Young remembers how in *Heatstroke*, before the filming, director Joe Gage instructed his actors to yell out "cum shot!" before they climaxed, and the cameraman would redirect his focus to them (Young 1991). The cum shot is one of the most important parts of the pornographic film. In the trade, it is often referred to as the "money shot."

Linda Williams has written extensively on the "money shot" in her book *Hardcore*. She puts forth some very astute observations regarding the cum shot's importance in the genre. It is "the visual evidence of the mechanical 'truth' of bodily pleasure caught in involuntary spasm; the ultimate and uncontrollable–the ultimate *because* uncontrollable–confession of sexual pleasure in the climax of orgasm" (Williams 1989, p. 101). It is the moment to which the male viewer relates and empathizes. The actor's spending signals the viewer's spending.

Williams continues with her analysis:

> The money shot is thus an obvious perversion–in the literal sense of the term, as a swerving away from more "direct" forms of genital engagement–of the tactile sexual connection. It substitutes for the relation between the actors the more solitary (and literally disconnected) visual pleasure of the male performer and the male viewer. (Ibid.)

Although Williams's assessment of the money shot is astute, it is necessary to take it a step further–not to discount her earlier analysis, but rather to allow for a further reassessment of the cum shot's representational value.

AIDS AND THE TRADE

It is not much of a secret that the current methods of sexual interaction (whether homosexual or heterosexual) have been greatly affected by the AIDS crisis. Within the gay community, safe sex is a relatively standard procedure. I mentioned earlier the late-coming representation of condom use in gay male porn videos. One of the reasons for this delay is the filmic trope of the cum shot. Once, this shot served purely as a signifier of male pleasure. In the decade of the epidemic, it also serves as a signifier of safe sex (Patton 1991). Pulling out before orgasm reduces the risk of HIV infection. Of course the argument can be made that currently, with widespread condom use in porn videos, it is unnecessary to pull out. The possibility always remains, though, of breaks or leaks in the condom. Safe sex activists and medical experts still strongly promote withdrawal before ejaculation. Thus, the exterior orgasm, the visual cum shot, must now also be regarded as proof of safe sex–a sort of erotic disclaimer that lives were not jeopardized on the set of the film. The cum shot remains, of course, Williams's "'truth' of bodily pleasure," but when standard sexual norms no longer hold up in the face of AIDS it is necessary to withdraw such misnomers as "perverse." The money shot may very well save lives, and its use in the past may very well be the reason many gay porn stars are alive today.

The subject of safe sex in gay male pornography is problematic. To suggest that depictions of unsafe sex in videos advocate such practices to the viewing audience is to fall into the censorious Robin Morgan WAP-trap ideology of porn begetting violent or unsafe behavior. There is, of course, no data to support this tenet. On the other hand, on the set, many directors, fearful that safe sex videos will not sell, often monetarily coerce young performers to engage in unsafe practices. It is sometimes the case that these actors are economically destitute; theirs is a hand-to-mouth existence in which the threat of future illness or death does not matter in light of their immediate struggles. Such exploitation is slowly abating within the industry.

Some directors choose to ignore unsafe practices on their set. J. D. Slater, self-appointed "bad boy of porn," says of his role as gay pornographer:

> As far as safe sex in my work is concerned, I will not preach or morally judge. I am simply a documentarian of sexual incidents. What an actor does is completely his own decision. I let an actor do exactly what he wants any way he wants to do it. Some directors think it's their job to instruct the public on safe sex, and for them, that's great, but that's not my responsibility. (1990, p. 26)

Slater goes on to say: "I used poppers in *Motorsexual* [1989, Le Salon] deliberately–to be as politically incorrect as possible, to do everything one wasn't supposed to in 30 seconds" (Ibid., p. 30).* It is not the effect Slater's videos may have on the viewing public which is of concern, but rather the effect his on-set ideologies have on his coworkers and performers. What one is seeing with *Motorsexual* and other Slater videos is the eroticization of a porn star's ignorance or daredevilry; at the risk of exaggeration, they are snuff films of sorts. Slater even eschews the "unsafe sex sells" excuse, believing he is documenting a "real-life" individual's decision as it is made in the context of the filming of a porn movie.

On January 24, 1992, I addressed the issue of unsafe sex in current gay porn in a paper delivered at the New York University symposium *Explicit Sex: Art or Phallacy?* The paper is entitled "Laying the Saints: Toward the Queer Canonization of Gay Male Porn Stars Dead From AIDS," and it serves as an intellectualized emotional apotropaic. Stressing the fact that unsafe sex will probably continue to exist in gay porn to some degree, I opt to recast the role of the porn stars involved from that of unsafe practitioner to that of martyred saint–one who practices for me what I can no longer enjoy. If I am unable to alter their behavior, I can at least

---

*Poppers (amyl nitrite) are purported to severely weaken the body's immune system.

reinterpret it. There are, of course, many ways to deal with the AIDS debacle; mine, perhaps, is no more radical than Slater's–although, as an industry outsider, I have less ability to influence the practices of the performers. Slater and the other directors who peddle high-risk activity are, of course, not directly responsible for the behavior of their stars. It would seem, however, to be economically fruitful to take a keener interest in their performers' health and well-being.

Fortunately there are gay porn-makers carrying on the tradition of Al Parker, who showed a decided interest in safe sex representations. Parker had a filmic field day creating new and kinky ways in which to have safe sex. In *Turbo Charge* (1988, Surge Studios/Vidco) he introduced his viewers to the protective use to which cellophane wrap can be put while rimming someone's ass (sort of a handy household variation of the dental dam). This particular scene was actually part of a three-minute safe sex video the Swiss AIDS Foundation commissioned from Parker. Subsequently, he incorporated the scene into a full-length feature video.

Parker also appended his videos with self-made public service announcements in which he addresses the issue of safe sex. On-camera, seated behind a desk, Parker asks why the viewer patronizes companies which promote unsafe practices. This patronage, he explains, buys such producers Ferraris at the fatal expense of their performers (Parker 1990). In 1987 and 1988 (the year of *Turbo Charge*), safe sex was still a hard sell. Parker directly challenges the viewers' conceptions of the erotic in this tag. Although Parker's company, Surge, had not fared well economically in the last few years of his life, representations of safe sex now exist almost throughout the entirety of current gay porn videos. Many video companies employ the porn stars themselves to give brief safe sex reminders prior to the film. Catalina has utilized the talents of Scott Bond, Lex Baldwin, and Cody Foster, and the informational prologues to BIC Productions' videos present two hunky C.H.P. officers who make it sound like you'll be issued a ticket if you do not follow their safe sex guidelines.

In discussing these two dichotomous forerunners of porn direction in the age of AIDS it is interesting to note that Slater, in an interview with *Edge* magazine, actually compares himself to Parker: "Of the people who started with me in the business, there's me and Al Parker–we're the last of the dinosaurs" (1990. p. 26). Slater callously predicts extinction. Parker, however, unlike his contemporary, was a fighter and evolver, capable of adapting to new sexual climates. Gay men, in general, have reconstructed their sexual habits as well, in light of AIDS. Some, like Slater, appear to embrace their impending fin-de-siècle extinction.

I do not want to sound proscriptive of men like Slater. But in watching how the industry has evolved and changed its perceptions of sex, it is devastating to look upon the "documentation" of, and by, someone like Slater, and see how far we have yet to go, especially in light of recent polls which illustrate an alarming increase in unprotected sex among teenagers, gay and straight, in the United States.

Most people involved in the gay male porn industry tend to follow safe sex guidelines. Off-film, however, it is impossible to say to what extent these actors incorporate safe sex into their escort services. Most of these models use the porn videos as self-promotion, advertisements of sorts, for their prostitution. Clients, having seen the stars in videos, can usually find them listed in the escort service sections of such magazines as the *Advocate*, *Edge*, *Frontiers*, and other similar gay-oriented metropolitan publications. The more famous the actor, the more money he can charge per session. Typical fees for a street prostitute range from $50 to $100 per hour. Porn star fees start at about $200 per hour, and top at an hourly rate of up to $1,000 (Parker 1990).

Unable to accurately assess the incidence of safe sex within these sessions, I tend to believe that most of these models are fairly conscientious about its employment. On a recent visit to Los Angeles, I was on the patio of West Hollywood's Astro Burger, a popular hustling site on Santa Monica Boulevard. This location is primarily frequented by young boys turning tricks with older men, though occasionally female prostitutes operate there as well. It is primarily a drive-by service. The boys cruise the motorists, and frequently get picked up. Eating at Astro Burger and waiting at the bus stop are successful ploys for keeping the police off their backs.

During the short time I was there, two prostitutes (a young white male and a young black female) sat talking about the trade. In terms of prostitution economics, these two subsist at a low level. At one point during their conversation, the girl asked the guy if he had an extra condom she could have. He then pulled out a handful of safe sex packets (two condoms, non-oxynol 9 lubricant, and safe sex instruction booklet) and gave her one, saying he never goes anywhere without them; a promising incident, indicative, one hopes, of condom deployment throughout the industry.

The gay porn industry is also addressing the AIDS crisis in other off-film ways. On November 7, 1990, Colt Studio held a benefit party for Northern Lights Alternatives (a Los Angeles program serving the HIV-affected community) at the Arena nightclub. On hand were popular Colt models. Michael Pereyra, model and International Mr. Leather 1988, hosted the evening. Other models signed autographs. Five life-size Colt Studio photographic prints were auctioned off, for $500 to $1,000 each. The party and auction proceeds (totalling over $18,000) were all donated to the charity.

Porn star Ryan Idol also strives to benefit the HIV-affected community through his public appearances: "At all my nightclub appearances, we do some kind of fundraising for AIDS. That is, if the owners go along with it. Eighty percent of them do" (1991, p. 42). Idol insinuates that the other 20 percent of the clubs are heterosexually oriented; in which case he would dance and strip for a primarily all-female audience.

Porn superstar Jeff Stryker donated his time to the Design Industries Foundation For AIDS (DIFFA) fundraising gala Love Ball 2, held May 22, 1991 at Manhattan's Roseland nightclub. Stryker, seated between Susan Sarandon and Fran Lebowitz, was one of many celebrity judges whose job it was to select the winning "house" of high-fashion voguers. Porn stars Richard Locke and Glenn Swann have both written safe sex books. Locke has authored *In the Heat of Passion: How to Have Hotter, Safer Sex* and Swann, with erotic fiction author John Preston, penned *Safe Sex: The Ultimate Erotic Guide*. Other porn stars devote their time to similar causes aiding the gay communities: the late porn star Jake Corbin was an active member of New York's ACT UP, and Chris Burns, who holds black belts in kung-fu and judo and has experience in karate, tai-kwon-do, jujitsu, and American boxing, recently made a video concerning anti-gay and -lesbian violence. Entitled *Take Back the Night*, it is a videotaped beginner's course in street self-defense for lesbians and gay men, emphasizing the most common methods of violent attack and the most effective ways to counter them.

The above are just a few examples of the gay male porn industry manifesting its social conscience, outside of videos, in relation to situations that erode its very foundations. These are instances of the industry addressing deplorable conditions which threaten its very existence, both within the business itself and within the viewing public which supports the business economically.

By demonstrating safe sex, these videos and their makers are offering not merely an educational prescription, but a necessity for the perpetuation of the gay male porn industry. Safe sex keeps the actors alive. It may very well teach the viewers new methods which may keep them alive, which in turn allows for the continuation of their video purchasing, thus keeping the industry alive. For many of these men, making porn videos is not enough; through their works outside the industry (yet capitalizing on their success in it) they are able to further extend the benefits of their life-affirming tenets. Although fantasy cannot eradicate AIDS and other threats, some of the fantasy-makers are doing their best.

* * *

The non-pornographic appearances of porn stars in the public sector serve the gay communities' construction of popular memory well. The performers embellish the representations of sexual fantasy and historistical rewriting with real-life examples of social conscience and awareness of their public. Stryker, Corbin, Burns, and others, extend the importance of gay porn as popular memory from passive optic/cerebral message to social action. Films such as *Screwing Screw Ups* and *Madness & Method* document the porn industry's machinations and present a view of the profession more realistic than the fictionalized accounts in *The Next Valentino* or *Sex, Lies, and Video Cassettes*. The documentaries allow the usually hidden profession of gay pornographer an historic viability and a place in the gay culture's popular memory, while extra-pornographist actions by the stars permit the industry to exceed its historio-fantasy limitations and personally interact with the gay communities.

Chapter VI

Hot and Bothered: Eroto-Political Porn

There are of course other ways to view gay male video pornography than those presented here. I have somewhat ennobled the genre–perhaps invested it with qualities some may find unapparent or nonexistent. I intend only to put forth a new model within which one might differently regard gay male porn videos. By doing so, however, I do not mean to imply that the whole of gay male video porn is a monolithically positive entity. As discussed earlier, there are many inherent problems within this industry and its productions. Racism, ageism, unsafe sex–all of these seem to work against the gay male communities. Their representations in porn videos reflect the shortcomings, the flaws within the culture. But it is from these same unflattering representations that we can learn and continue to evolve.

Porn videos are manifestations of gay male popular memory. They document many aspects of our current condition and rewrite the history from which we have been excluded. Porn videos are a "dimension of political practice" (Popular Memory Group 1982, p. 205). They exemplify the politics of visibility, putting society's unseeable, unknowable, unspeakable histories where they can be seen, known, and heard by those willing to receive them. Of gay pornography, Michael Bronski states:

> In a world that denies the very existence of homosexuality and homosexual desires, gay pornography performs two vital functions. It depicts sexual desire, bringing it out of the mind and into the reality of the material world. Porn becomes a sexual object. The sexual identity of the viewer is consequently reinforced, bolstered by the fact that the viewer has been engaged by, and responded to, a sexual object. (1984, p. 161)

In this model, gay porn can be seen as a political tool, a means of strengthening the troops, manning the ranks, as it were. Through its reinforcement of the viewer's sexual identity, porn encourages gay men's self-acceptance, and perhaps mobilizes them to (homo)sex-positive action.

Nevertheless, what gay porn does not do, for the most part, is mobilize gay men for more overt political action. Making one's gay self visible is, indeed, a political move. Fighting to maintain and further this sense of visibility is the next step in the gay rights movement, but one which is not often promoted or, indeed, documented by porn video. If gay porn videos are to continue to succeed as historical documents, as accounts of gay popular memory, they now need to evolve further, to become political in more overt and aggressive ways. There are a few good examples of gay porn which succeed in the documentation of the new gay activism. Perhaps, to some viewers, they may even serve as a call to action.

SEXUALLY ACTIVE ACTIVISTS

Gay Men's Health Crisis (GMHC) has produced two gay male hardcore safe sex short videos: *Midnight Snack* and *Law and Order* (both 1990). Essentially apolitical, the importance of these films lies in the fact that they were produced by a political organization rather than a porn production company. GMHC has always been aware of the educational potential of erotica. Their explicit safe sex comics, photo-illustrated pamphlets of correct condom use, sensual propagandistic posters, and these videos are all examples of this working knowledge of "pop" erotica.

In *Midnight Snack*, ACT UP activist Peter Staley demonstrates the tasteful uses to which a condom can be put. Staley covers his partner's sheathed erection with various ice cream confections, and then licks it clean. Staley's partner even sends a political message via his haircut: his head is shaved, leaving only an inverted triangular patch of hair, which is dyed pink. The pink triangle, a gay activist symbol appropriated from Nazi Germany, is often accompanied by the phrase "silence = death."

Law and Order, a safe fistfucking video, incorporates two leathermen (porn stars Keith Ardent and Joe Simmons), the former dressed as a cop. Both *Midnight Snack* and *Law and Order* are interesting also because they pair up a black man and a white man, without their titles signalling that they are to be relegated to a racial subgenre. These videos demonstrate a racial equality unpracticed by most other porn videos. Not only do these two films serve as safe sex education and as examples of racial equality and integration within the gay communities, but they are also produced and distributed by a "politically correct" organization–a movement not motivated by capital gains, but by health and political reformational goals.

Josh Eliot's video *Object of Desire* (1990, Catalina) is an example of the gay porn industry's first attempt to subliminally propagate political awareness, very much in the style of GMHC's *Midnight Snack*. The final scene in *Object of Desire* revolves around one man's futuristic glory-hole fantasy. He is led by a cloaked guide into a black room illuminated only by a large fluorescent pink triangle on the wall. Several penises then appear through various triangular glory holes in the wall. The man proceeds to give blow jobs to all of them. Here again the pink triangle as political symbol is subtly employed. The pink triangle has worked its way into the gay community's consciousness through its overwhelming public visibility. Now it is being incorporated into porn videos, to be seen by the porn viewing markets which may not have ready access to information regarding such overt political symbols and movements (remember Oklahoma, the country's largest mail-order gay porn market). The pink triangle which symbolizes the gay movement toward sexual liberation and freedom is thus explicitly and intrinsically linked with the most visible means of the representation of gay male sexual practice. It is a link which has long been understood by most gay men, and here, it is visually represented for the benefit of yet more gay men.

Busted (1991, Stryker Productions) is another somewhat political video, in that it addresses the porn industry's consternation with unwarranted attacks and arrests by the FBI. The opening roll-crawl (which is vocally embellished by Stryker) denounces the FBI's raids on the porn industry and outrightly calls for a change in the American government.* The film then follows the exploits of two closet-

---

*See Appendix A for a complete citation of this roll-crawl, in both its written and narrated versions.

case agents staking out Stryker in the hopes of nabbing him during his next film shoot. They end up busting him in the course of an orgiastic party and carting the superstar away. The viewer is led to believe there will be a sequel to this video in which he finds out what happens to Stryker. The film, in its indictment of the false pieties of government law enforcement, also reflects the growing pride among sex workers in general–a pride which, more and more, demands public legitimation, not unlike the gay communities themselves. *Busted* exposes the sexual hypocrisies of the typical American. The two FBI agents who bust Stryker are also big fans of his. No doubt, in the sequel, Stryker will have these two feds begging for his dick. Stryker's punchline will be a literal fucking over of the oppressive, sex-negative American government.

One other video worthy of mention for having its eroto-politics in the right place, is *Jumper* (1992, HIS Video). The title character, played by Ryan Yeager, is an angel (once a Revolutionary War soldier) who comes back to Earth to teach West Hollywood gay men a few gay-positive, sex-positive lessons. Jumper teaches a self-hating closet-case about pride, helps a shy nerd come out, and embraces safe sex techniques in each encounter, leaving behind condom gift-packs after each session. The ending is a mawkish treatment of the effects of homophobia, in which Jumper's favorite Earth trick winds up an angel after a fatal fag-bashing. The two are then joined eternally as lovers in heaven. Whereas the rest of the movie attempts to apotropaically minister to some of the problems with which gay men must cope, this final scene is merely maudlin, offering only the cliche of Christlike ascension to heaven as compensation for unpardonable acts of mortal homophobia on Earth. Both *Jumper* and *Sex Shooters II* (discussed in Chapter III) attempt to reach a porno-political milestone by addressing the issue of anti-gay hate crimes. The erotic and sexual solutions put forth by these videos, however, fall short. Porn, although about many things, is based upon sex, and sex can answer only so many problems. Fag-bashing, obviously, is not one of them.

A QUEER CONSCIENCE

In recent years, the gay movement has splintered into many different factions, one of the most volatile and visible being those who identify with the word "Queer" as opposed to "gay." The chief distinction between the two camps is that Queers are anti-assimilationist; they do not want to be thought of as "just like straights." They revel in their difference. Queers reject the Castro clone persona and the internalized homophobia of self-appellations such as "straight-acting" and "straight-appearing." Opting instead for a more unique and "in-your-face" style of self-expression, Queers often incorporate tattoos, bodily piercings, scarification, and couture amalgams of punk, drag, leather, and hip-hop. Their confrontational politics (immediately indicated by the appropriation of the word "queer," and the consequent new spin on its traditional negative implications) are best exemplified by the Queer Nation movement, as well as the recent proliferation of incendiary photocopied publications commonly known as 'zines.

Queers have not been readily embraced by the gay porn industry. In fact, the very idea of "gay" is not very prevalent in the genre. There is a noticeable dearth of porn videos with gay-indicative titles. Male-indicative, dick-indicative, and fetish-indicative titles comprise the norm. John Rowberry (1991) catalogues only two video titles that run contrary to this norm: the campily *sturm und drang*, throb-and-drip *Gayracula* (1983, HIS Video) and *Queer: The Movie* (1990, Live Video). The latter, directed by Christopher Rage, does not incorporate either the politics or the presentational aesthetics of the Queer movement. Rather, Rage has appropriated the word because its confrontational connotations exemplify the confrontational sexual subject matter of his art.

The reasons behind the lack of gay-implicative video titles seem obvious. In an industry where many of the customers are in the closet, or depend upon secrecy and discretion, such titles blow the whistle. Marketers reach a much wider audience with less identifying, and therefore less intimidating, video titles. While viewing the videos is a very private experience, the consumer is linked more publicly to the titles (whether through computer order lists or at the video rental check-out counter). The content of the videos can be (and is increasingly) gay-positive, homo-political, or even Queer. Titles, however, are still deemed to require discretion.

The Queer porn video, as a subgenre of its own, is slowly coming into being. One of the earliest examples of Queer porn is the film

Motorpunks (1991, AVG). The video professes no politics, but the bodily presentations of the boys (many tattoos and piercings), coupled with a radical leathersexuality (minus the mock-seriousness and ritualism of much s/m porn), most definitely preach the new Queer perspective.

The most influential and artistic Queer movie to date is Bruce LaBruce's *No Skin Off My Ass* (1991, J.D.s and Associates). The film (loosely structured after Robert Altman's *That Cold Day in the Park*) chronicles the romance between two Queer men, one of which, as an act of symbolic political appropriation against the homophobia of supremacist skinheads, has himself adopted the skinhead coiffure. Although not essentially pornographic, *No Skin Off My Ass* does incorporate several instances of explicit Queer sex, replete with hard-ons and cum shots. These scenes are presented in a very rough filmic fashion, reminiscent of the gay underground. LaBruce's film is a seminal piece of what should, hopefully, prove to be the burgeoning Queer cinema. Perhaps a distinct Queer porn movement, picking up where *Motorpunks* left off, is soon to follow.

CUMMING AND COMING OUT

In earlier essays on this same topic, I called for a gay male pornography that celebrates our sexual practices at the same time that it celebrates our new political activism. For example, in an unpublished essay written in May of 1990, I suggested possible video narratives in which gay men might meet at ACT UP demonstrations and subsequently go home to have hot, safe sex. Since that time, one video has been released which satisfies these expectations.

More of a Man (1990, All Worlds Video) is a strange but gratifying video. It pleases erotically, and titillates politically. It opens with Vito (Joey Stefano), a straight Italian construction worker, in a Catholic church adorned with many votive candles. He clutches a rosary while giving an opening monologue to God, asking for guidance because of his strange and sinful thoughts. In the next scene, Vito enters the men's room of a bus stop and occupies one of the stalls. There is a glory hole in the partition between stalls. Above the hole, in the unoccupied stall, there is a "Silence = Death"/pink triangle decal. Actor Michael Parks enters this stall. He and Joey then have a mutual suck and fuck scene. Both use condoms during the anal intercourses. Throughout these sex scenes, Vito's rosary is always visible, dangling from his back pocket. Outside the stalls Parks tells Vito that he's a natural-born piece of ass and that he would love to fuck him again. Vito, insulted, punches Parks in the mouth, calls him a "faggot" and leaves.

In the following scene, Vito walks into a bar and joins his friend Belle (drag queen Chi Chi LaRue). They have a drink and talk about his "problem" with homosexual men–they just won't leave him alone. Belle rolls her eyes, indicating that she knows Vito is deluding himself. But she is patient. There is a new bartender, Duffy (Michael Henson). He wears a Dodgers cap and Dodgers T-shirt. The three of them talk about Duffy's first anniversary, for which he is headed, champagne and roses in hand. Vito asks Belle if she has ever met Duffy's "old lady," to which Belle replies, "Who says it's his old lady? Maybe it's his old man." Vito, flabbergasted, responds, "You think so? Nah, he's a Dodgers fan." Belle rolls her eyes again.

Cut to a bedroom scene. Close-up of Duffy's face, framed by lit candles–an obvious echo of the first scene of Vito in church. Duffy is regarding something with a slightly reverential gaze. A cut to a point-of-view shot looking through the candles reveals what Duffy sees: three posters–the first, of the pink triangle with the words "Silence = Death" below it; the second, artist Keith Haring's poster for National Coming Out Day; and the third, the least familiar, merely stating "Fight For The Living." The camera then pulls back to reveal Duffy and his lover (Butch Taylor) nude, in bed. They begin a slow, sensual, romantic lovemaking session. This is interrupted by a phone call, which they monitor through the answering machine. It is Dave, an acquaintance from ACT UP; he really needs to talk to Duffy. Duffy does not answer the call. The two resume their lovemaking. The lover is about to insert his unprotected penis up Duffy's butt (are we to assume they have both been tested?), when Dave rings again. Duffy's lover, frustrated, gets up and goes to the kitchen. He is tired of these constant interruptions from Duffy's political friends. Duffy follows him into the kitchen; they resume their lovemaking. Duffy fucks his lover (using a condom). It was supposed to be Duffy, though, who gets fucked, since it has been such a long time since that has happened in their relationship.

After the fucking, the partner expresses his worries that Duffy's love has waned ever since Duffy became a "professional homosexual" (i.e., an ACT UPer). They return to the bedroom and open the champagne. The phone rings again, and Duffy answers it. The lover threatens to leave Duffy if Duffy does not hang up the phone. Duffy refuses to be ordered around. The lover douses Duffy with the champagne and walks out. This relationship is over. The lover is clearly presented as immature, politically lethargic, and not worthy of Duffy's attentions.

Back in the bar, Vito and Belle are drinking champagne in celebration of Belle's new singing gig at a West Hollywood bar. Duffy walks in and relates the story of his breakup. Vito, astounded by Duffy's homosexuality, does a double take. Belle says sarcastically, "Yeah, he's a Dodgers fan." Vito, uncomfortable, leaves. Duffy is shocked that Vito denies his own homosexuality. Belle says he is learning; he'll come around soon.

In the next scene, Vito gets a tattoo to make him feel more macho. When the tattoo is finished, he gives the artist (Rick Donovan) a blow job. The artist then charges him $50 for the work. Vito, evidently having thought the blow job would get him a freebie, storms out furiously, calling the artist "the sickest motherfucker I ever met," to which the tattoo artist calmly responds: "Second. You came first." Vito puts a brick through the shop window.

Back in the bar, Belle is reading a letter from, she tells the bartender, her son. Close-up of a photo of a little boy; on the back is written, "To Daddy, thank you for the Nintendo game. Love, Jimmy." The viewer realizes Belle is not the "real" woman Vito thinks, but either a drag queen or (less likely) a transsexual. Vito enters, showing off his manly new tattoo. Belle proceeds to dispel the masculinist myth of tattoos by revealing hers, and by telling Vito that Duffy has a tattoo as well. Vito is crestfallen.

That night, Vito is cruising in his pickup truck. He picks up a blonde female prostitute, Mindy. They park, and she gives him a blow job. He has a little trouble getting it up at first. But everything works all right when he starts fantasizing that it is Duffy who is sucking him. The scene cuts back and forth–now it is Mindy performing fellatio on Vito, now Duffy. In the fantasy cuts, Vito then goes down on Duffy (we are not shown whether Vito is really going down on Mindy). He is brought out of his reverie by Mindy, who is wiping Vito's cum from her mouth and asking to be driven back.

Later, Vito is home, smoking in bed. A crucifix hangs above him. He talks to God again: "Look, I don't mean to be a pain in the ass, but let's face it, we've got a real problem here, you know. Like, I've been having these impure thoughts again, and they're getting worse, you know. I been thinking a lot about, well, about this certain person . . . " Who could it be?

Next day, Vito is knocking on a door. Duffy (of course) opens it. Now he is wearing an ACT UP baseball cap with his Dodgers shirt. Vito is dropping off ten dollars that Belle owed Duffy. Duffy invites him inside. We see the three posters on the wall again. Duffy is in the middle of making demonstration posters. The two enjoy some light sexual banter. Duffy grabs Vito's ass (whereupon Vito's rosary falls out); Vito responds by pushing Duffy to the ground and leaving (forgetting the rosary).

Next, a short scene of Belle on the phone with Vito, making sure he will attend her performance that night. She says she has written "a special opening for the act" just for him.

That night, Vito enters the club (called Another World). Duffy is filling in as a bartender. He gives Vito back his rosary and invites him to be on the club's Gay Pride Parade float the following day. Vito declines. Belle takes the stage (actually, sits on the piano) and introduces the special opening, saying: "It kind of tells a story. It kind of tells him he's more of a man than he thinks he is." The song turns out to be a very clever (for porn writing) and gay-positive twist on masculine myths extolling the presence of gays in all walks of life, and celebrating their pride, dignity, and strength in coping with the injustices handed down by a heterosexist society.* Vito gets a little choked up by this gay-affirming life story, but not so much that he is unable to cruise three guys sitting at the bar (Lonn Flexx, Chris McKenzie, and Mathieu Rollins). The four of them have sex in front of all the bar patrons, including Belle and Duffy. After the four have finished, Belle comes over to Vito (who is lying, dazed and confused), says "Love ya, honey," and kisses him. Vito then talks to

---

*See Appendix B for transcript of the song "More of a Man."

God yet again, telling him he is seriously considering attending the next day's Gay Pride Parade.

Cut to scenes of the parade's preparation. Vito wanders among such real-life participants as The Spike bar's float, the USC limo, and Dykes on Bikes. Finally, he sees Duffy and Belle on their float, cruising down Santa Monica Boulevard. With the help of Duffy, he hops on. The two hold hands a little longer than is heterosocially acceptable. Duffy leads Vito into the float's interior: a cozy little nook with a round mattress. Amid mounting sexual tension, they caress and kiss (Vito's first kiss in the movie). After a lot of mutual, reciprocal foreplay, Vito asks who is to fuck whom first. Duffy allows Vito to start (a big move for him, too), and asks Vito to pass him a rubber, to which Vito naively replies: "No, it's against my religion." (Vito, or the director, seems to have forgotten that he employed a rubber in the first scene; but better that script continuity be neglected for the safety of the actors.) Duffy insists that condoms are not against *his* religion, and Vito complies. Vito fucks Duffy. What follows is a great moment of sexual realism not found in most other gay porn videos. While getting fucked, Duffy blindly gropes around the mattress's edges, trying to locate another condom, so he can fuck Vito. He finds one, tears open the package, and puts it on without missing a beat. It is a very real-life situation to which most gay men can easily relate; unfortunately scenes like this are rarely incorporated into films. The two men switch positions and finish up, to the accompaniment of loud and continuous parade-spectator applause from outside the float. They kiss, dress, and return topside. The last shot of the film is a freeze frame of a used rubber next to Vito's discarded rosary.

I have described *More of a Man* at such length for several reasons. First, it is the best example of current gay pornography documenting the sexual politics of the modern gay rights movement. As cited earlier, the Popular Memory Group asserts that "the recreation of popular struggles shows us that [oppressed groups] *do* make history" (1982, p. 212). Depictions such as those in *More of a Man* of the struggles of coming out, gay liberation, and AIDS activism are described herein as a vital and necessary next step in the representations of gay pornography. Second, *More of a Man* also attempts, quite earnestly, to dispel the masculinist and heterosexist myths surrounding the "gay male vs. straight male" debate. And last, this video functions more than adequately as erotica.

Unlike any other gay male video, *More of a Man* constructs its narrative around a young man's dual coming out: sexual as well as political. Currently, the very act of coming out is essentially political; at the very least, it is highly politicized by activist groups. In *More of a Man* Vito finds solace in the politically correct arms of another man. This is the man for which he will leave behind his destructive acts of hatred (psychoanalytically read as self-hatred redirected at others like him), and his Catholicism—whose leaders are responsible for the propagation of many prejudicial and hetero-sexist social standards. This video also serves as a recruitment commercial of sorts for ACT UP and other gay-positive groups and movements—a message which, until now, has only been implied or suggested in other films. The viewer cannot miss the proliferation of activist symbols throughout this video, and their juxtaposition with symbols of Catholicism never lets the viewer forget the struggle between AIDS and gay activists and the church. This conflict is addressed through both symbols and actions: It is suggested that Vito's Catholic upbringing is the source of much of his self-loathing and, thus, his violence; and the discarded used condom and discarded rosary remark, in no uncertain (however symbolic) terms, upon his new-found sexual freedom.

More of a Man also breaks down American myths of the macho straight male. Straight men have no monopoly on tattoos, the Dodgers, romantic evenings of champagne and roses, or for that matter, the fathering of children. This video asserts that gay men too take pleasure in those activities that are, by social definition, exclusively heterosexual. Belle's song (written by director Jerry Douglas and also entitled "More of a Man") is a paean to the presence of gay men in society, addressed to Vito and to homophobic men, gay or straight, everywhere. The song tells them gay men are their doctors and lawyers; gay men demand and deserve respect. And sung by a drag queen, the final line of the song really hits a strong gay-positive note: "I'm more of a woman than you'll ever have, and more of a man than you'll ever be." This is heavy affirmative action for a fuck flick, and from a comic relief drag queen.

The one serious shortcoming from which I think the video suffers is its omission of racial integration. All the boys are white; men of color are nowhere to be seen. Aside from this neglect, the video successfully documents the various levels of sexual and social practice gay men enjoy: the anonymity of a glory hole; the pleasure of a little pain (manifested in the tattooing); multiple partners; silly attempts to prove oneself straight; true love; failed love (another rarity in fantasy representations); drag; AIDS activism; and coming out. For these things are all inextricably webbed together in gay men's lives. The video attempts to lead the way toward a revisionist gay pornography. *More of a Man*, self-consciously aware of its role in (and as) gay male popular memory, proves that pornography can more fully integrate social realities into its fantasy sexual representations.

The question arises, though, as to what effect overt politicization has on the erotic efficacy of these films. Do the various activist symbols, political plot lines, and agit-prop entertainment detract from *More of a Man*'s masturbatory intent? Or can erotics and politics harmonize within such skin flicks? Certain issues in the past few years surrounding *More of a Man* seem destined to address, if not answer, these questions. The 1990 *Adult Video News* Awards* (held in January, 1991 at the Consumer Electronics Show in Las Vegas) named the film Best Gay Video of the Year; Joey Stefano was named Best Actor; Chi Chi LaRue was cited for Best Non-Sexual Performance; director Jerry Douglas won the award for Best Screenplay. The *AVN* judges praised *More of a Man* for "rais[ing] the adult feature into the realm of cinematic art without sacrificing the sexual intensity" (quoted in Wockner 1991). For these judges–experts in their field–the political content of the video did not deter the traditional orgasmic enjoyment.

Political content may also be a legally saving grace for adult videos. On February 14, 1991, in a random vice sweep, *More of a Man* was confiscated from Chicago's Bijou Theater (the oldest gay theater in the country, and the only gay theater in the Midwest) by police on obscenity charges. Theater manager Lonnie Hill was also taken into custody (and released on $1,000 bond nine hours later).

---

*The *AVN* Awards honor both gay and straight videos, each treated as a separate category.

Subsequently, Lieutenant Earl Nevels of the Chicago Police Department's Vice Control section "'assign[ed] an investigator' to obtain search and seizure orders for all stores carrying the movie. After that's done, he said he will consider ordering additional raids on video stores to look for more all-male X-rated films" (Olson 1991). At work in this case are many different and difficult levels of politics. First, there is an obvious antigay bias promoting these actions. Second, there is possibly a violation by the police department of the free-speech provisions of the First Amendment to the U.S. Constitution. The obscenity charges are difficult to prove. Under Illinois Revised Statutes Chapter 38, Paragraph 11-20, material or performance is "obscene" if:

> (1) the average person, applying contemporary adult community standards, would find that, taken as a whole, it appeals to prurient interests; and (2) the average person, applying contemporary adult community standards, would find that it depicts or describes, in a patently offensive way, ultimate sexual acts or sadomasochistic sexual acts, whether normal or perverted, actual or simulated, or masturbation, excretory functions or lewd exhibition of the genitals; and (3) taken as a whole, it lacks serious literary, artistic, political or scientific value. (Ibid.)

The political content of the film led one of the Bijou's two lawyers, Jane Whicher, to believe that the obscenity charges would be defeated; the serious message, the safe sex, and the representation of AIDS activism perhaps bestow the necessary "serious literary, artistic, political or scientific value" upon *More of a Man*. The case's other defending lawyer, Burton Joseph, however, pointed to the slipperiness of the term "community standards" as the important factor. The "community" in question could be read as north Lakefront (very gay), the city as a whole, the state–or be as localized in its definition as patrons of the Bijou Theater. Joseph predicted the case would be thrown out of court on this question of "community" definition. On March 24, 1991, the obscenity charges against the Bijou Theater and *More of a Man* were indeed dropped.

Political content in porn films may necessarily be the next wave in the industry–especially if that is what is needed to combat the various misdirected interpretations of obscenity laws and the abuses of the free-speech Amendment. At the same time, the *Adult Video News* Awards indicate that overt political content does not necessarily undermine a film's sexual power and intent. For those viewers for whom it does, there is always the fast-forward button or the concession stand.

Chapter VII

Conclusion (aka–Cum Shot)

The manifestation of a social movement's popular memory is a valuable political tool. Earlier, and frequently, I referred to the Popular Memory Group's averment that popular memory is a dimension of political practice. For the gay rights movement, then, pornography (as popular memory) is a potentially valuable tool (though, to date, a mostly ignored one). Gay male video pornography works doubly well in destroying social truths which are often predicated upon the constructs of the social control of time and space. Porn videos deconstruct the social order's oppressive discourse of time and history. By documenting states of existence as they occur, gay videos capture aspects of gay male history as they happen. They are a history of sexuality, desire, environment, entertainment, fashion, and ideology. These videos also actively rewrite the American past, incorporating positive gay images into those historic domains from which gay men have been excluded. America's established historical truths are confounded by these homosexualist revisions. New versions of historical truth are put forth, very strongly and very visibly challenging the old.

Gay porn disrupts the social constructs of space on two levels: one immediate, and one metaphoric. The visibility of these videos in daily life immediately destroys the public/private dichotomy so cherished by heterosexist society. The videos, with their enticing box covers, can be seen in most video stores across the country, advertised on cable television, and displayed in store windows (especially in larger metropolitan centers such as New York, Los Angeles, and San Francisco). Gay pornography, in general, is also highly visible on newsstands and in bookstores everywhere. The sexual practices of gay men, a highly privatized (and marginalized) experience, are permeating the American public's consciousness via the mass dissemination and availability of gay porn.

In Manhattan's Forty-second Street/Times Square district there are numerous porn palaces, both gay and straight, coexisting peacefully. Male clients are able to frequent these theaters with relative anonymity, and satiate (to a degree) their various sexual fantasies. Even within the environs of the straight arcades, gay male porn flicks are occasionally offered in the private video booths. Such a coexistence allows clients to explore a polysexuality, as it were, within the safe construct of fantasy. In these theaters (and theater districts) men, regardless of their orientation, can push their limits via fantasy, without fear of disrupting their sexual "realities." Although not entirely politically correct within the framework of contemporary gay activism, these porn palaces are attempts at utopian spaces of polysexual entertainment and integration in the erotic imagination. In terms of actual practice and person-to-person contact, they fall short of gay activist ideals. Nonetheless, they are examples of the infiltration of gay male porn into traditionally straight male realms.

On a more metaphoric level, gay porn videos break down the public/private dichotomy through their representations of sex in public spaces or typically "heterosexual" spaces. The images of men fucking each other at the rodeo, in high school locker rooms, on the subway, or at the office, blur public/private boundaries. The fact that many gay men actually do participate in sex in public places (parks, rest stops, dark alleys) only helps to further this effect of spatial deconstruction. These videos demonstrate the violation (both wishful and actual) of public (and heterosexist) spaces by privatizing them, in a way. Porn puts gay men having gay sex in front of everyone's face, making it impossible to ignore and confuting the truths of the old regime. With this breakdown of time and space, gay porn helps to erode the "truth" of our abjection.

Gay porn videos thus actively abet the deconstruction of heterosexist social norms. As popular memory, they can only help implement the instatement of new gay-positive truths in this country. There are, of course, inherent problems which need amending; there are in any social movement. Yet it seems to me quite clear that gay male video pornography must be regarded separately from the state of pornography as a whole. To continue to compare it to heterosexual male-oriented porn is to go nowhere.

Of course there are those who would disagree. But in light of the different types of pornography, the ideologies of contemporary anti-pornography movements, like Women Against Pornography (WAP), Men Against Pornography (MAP), and Feminists Fighting Pornography, seem imprecise. To castigate all porn under the empirically unproven credo "pornography is the theory; rape, the practice" is to fail to see the potentialities of political progress through the appropriation and recodification of hegemonically subordinating practices. It is far more political and radical for gays and women to assert their sexuality via pornography than it is to attempt to eradicate its existence altogether. Women's and gays' sexual desires are already so largely silenced that to do away with means of sexually explicit representation altogether would only complete the silencing of our right to freedom of sexual expression. Pat Califia, in her article "Among Us, Against Us: The New Puritans," points out that:

> The chief result of closing down the porn industry would be to enhance sexual repression. People would have even less access to information about sex and erotic material than they do now. Homosexuals and other sexual minorities would lose a vital source of contact–the sex ads. It would be even more difficult for women, lesbians and other disenfranchised groups to circulate accurate information about their sexuality and create their own erotica. [1988, p. 23]

While straight porn does show that women are indeed sexual beings capable of desire and pleasure, their desires, pleasures, and gratifications are rarely dealt with honestly or fully. It is up to women, gay or straight, to accomplish that by producing their own porn. Filmmakers like Candida Royalle, Annie Sprinkle, and Fanny Fatale are breaking new ground in this area. They are constructing new sexual histories by, for, and about women in much the same way many gay male porn producers are.

Gay male porn, though, has also come under attack by such "feminist" coalitions as WAP and MAP. John Stoltenberg, head cheerleader for Men Against Pornography, declares that, whereas straight pornography is about misogyny (which it is, mostly), gay pornography is about homophobia as well as misogyny. This, I believe, is inaccurate. In "Gays and the Propornography Movement: Having the Hots for Sex Discrimination," Stoltenberg states:

> The values in the sex that is depicted in gay male sex films are very much the values in the sex that gay men tend to have. They are also, not incidentally, very much the values that straight men tend to have–because they are very much the values that male supremacists tend to have: taking, using, estranging, dominating–essentially, sexual power-mongering. [1990, p. 249]

What are these values of which he speaks? Disembodied hard-ons, impersonal commingling, close-ups of sexual penetration, "scenes of forced fellatio, assault and molestation, humiliation and exploitation, chaining and bondage, the violence interlarded among the allegedly noncoercive sucking and fucking" (Ibid.), to name a few. Stoltenberg insists that the egomaniacal power struggle of the masculine over the feminine which holds sway in the heterosexual world is mimicked in the sexual practices of gay men as well; after all, they are still men. Stoltenberg does a great disservice to the gay community. His notion that the "sexual power-mongering" evident in gay pornography reveals a redirected misogyny and an internalized homophobia is a right wing fantasy posing as radical politics. Stoltenberg, with his anti-gay-pornography ideologies, is aiding and abetting the silencing and marginalizing treatment gay men have been actively and visibly fighting against for over two decades. He allows the gay community no cultural autonomy. To borrow a concept from Brian Pronger's *The Arena of Masculinity*, there are two worlds, two mythic levels of existence and experience in contemporary American culture: the orthodox and the paradox (1990, pp. 63-81). In Pronger's model, heterosexuality and the dominance of the masculine over the feminine is the orthodox way of life in America. Homosexuality, then, is a paradox. These levels of existence and experience are based on the concept of gender and its ideologies of power. It is the random and unwarranted assertion of this power within the orthodoxy which inspires Pronger to use the word "mythic" here.

Gay men and women then, by process of living in a paradoxical situation, begin to destroy the power relations of gender to which heterosexuals so strictly adhere, and actively undermine the heterosexual orthodoxy through their sexual practices. In male homosexual sex, gay men wield "power" over other men (instead of women) at the same time as they allow themselves to be rendered "powerless" by men (like women are supposed to be in the orthodox world of sexuality). The gender power system breaks down in homosexual sex. Gay men embody both masculine and feminine traits, thereby disproving the constructed quality of absolute gender and gender roles. Orthodox sexuality's untruths are made visible, and when this occurs, new truths can be constructed and substituted.

Stoltenberg makes the mistake of viewing straight pornography and gay male pornography as a single entity, instead of granting them individual status. That which is bad, unfair, or misdirected in straight porn does not necessarily apply to gay porn. To view pornography as monolithic is to view the variety of sexual experiences as monolithic too. It also suggests that the myriad sexual fantasies gay men may enjoy (whether in real life or in filmic representations) are dictated by male supremacist values. Bondage, humiliation, and s/m, as long as they are consensual, are all legitimate sexual practices. For Stoltenberg to aver that these practices are politically incorrect or, indeed, self-hating is to practice the same male supremacist subjugational techniques he so avidly condemns.

All of this is not to say that the gay community does not harbor cases of internalized homophobia, or that its pornography is entirely free of negative images. Stoltenberg, in a reactionary and paranoid manner, refuses to see through the inherently objectifying lens of the camera into a world where many positive representations of, by, and for gay men exist.

Many of the pornutopian images in these videos are not necessarily fantasy, but rather, aspirations. Gay porn videos are not only erotic implements, but also political tools, political action. If utilized properly, in conjunction with other aspects of the gay rights movements (such as the Names Project AIDS Memorial Quilt, ACT UP, Queer Nation, GMHC, Gay Pride parades, and so forth), gay male pornographic videos may very well prove to be an effective method for getting us up, getting us off, and getting us through socially imposed barriers.

The study of gay male video pornography and its subsequent off-shoots (porn star political activism, for instance) allows access to a deeper understanding of the sexual, social, cultural, and psychic realities of the various gay communities, past and present. The continuing production of gay pornography is essential to the communities' well-being, for, as the Popular Memory Group stated, as a

> formation of popular memory [gay male video pornography] is one means by which an organic social group acquires a knowledge of the larger context of its collective struggles, and becomes capable of a wider transformative role in the society. Most important of all, perhaps, it is the means by which we may become self-conscious about the formation of our own common-sense beliefs, those that we appropriate from our immediate social and cultural milieu. These beliefs have a history and are also produced in determinate processes. The point is to recover their 'inventory,' not in the manner of the folklorist who wants to preserve quaint ways for modernity, but in order that, their origin and tendency known, they may be *consciously* adopted, rejected or modified. In this way a popular historiography, especially a history of the commonest forms of consciousness, is a necessary aspect of the struggle for a better world. [1982, p. 214]

The production and study of gay pornography is just one of many possible starting blocks from which to begin this political marathon toward a "better world" in which the diverse gay communities are of an equal status with the rest of society. An inventory of gay porn lists many positive and many negative attributes. Concessions must be made, with the understanding that there is the potential for rejection or modification of the less constructive qualities and manifestations of the genre. Accepting both the good with the bad, gay male pornography as popular memory affords viewers a multifaceted visual representation of gay male history, and, in its very production and perpetuation, it more often than not serves as a potent political action against the oppression of the patriarchy. It is necessary to acknowledge the instances of patriarchal echoes within gay pornography (i.e., racism, ageism, and internalized homophobia) and address them so that we may begin to eradicate them from our self-representations. The industry has begun to do this with the images of internalized homophobia prevalent during the mid-1980s. It should use this trend-reversing example as an empowering paradigmatic device for the further modification and subsequent sociopolitical success of the genre.

Jacking off to gay porn has never been so powerful as it is now. If it is understood and embraced that gay porn serves as popular memory, then every porn-induced queer orgasm is a political act, no matter how private. Each is a hot juicy wad metaphorically flying in the collective face of those who would attempt to further oppress the advancing gay communities, and clogging the synapses of their dominant memory.

Appendix A

Roll-crawl from *Busted* (1991, Stryker Productions). Written by Bob Milin. Directed by John Travis and Richard Harrison. "The Star-Spangled Banner" plays under the voice-over.

As written:

In the year 1991, the FBI made massive raids on the adult video industry. These raids focused on video distributors, bookstores and productions across the nation. Closing many business's [sic] and sending people to jail all for the sale and distribution of sex video tapes. The people of the nation are now faced with the government of the United States trying to dictate the sexual practices Americans should have. People are losing their rights to life, liberty, and the pursuit of happiness. We have to stand for our rights and fight like our forefathers did. This is the new sexual revolution, and like prohibition, time will pass and the government will realize they were wrong "again." That will be another step towards freeing America from the old laws, made when homosexuality was not even considered natural. Things have changed and if the government doesn't get with the system, then we should change the government. The world is confused. Sex lives are being censored. Now, the story continues.

As narrated, with ad libs, by Jeff Stryker:

In the year 1991, the FBI made massive raids on the adult video industry. These raids were focused on video distributors, bookstores and production across the nation. Closing many businesses and sending people to jail all for the sale and distribution of sex video tapes. The people of the nation are now faced with the government of the United States trying to dictate the sexual practices Americans should have. People are losing their rights to life, liberty, and the pursuit of happiness by a bunch of old shits that have lived their lives and had their fun. Damn it, we stand for our rights and we have to fight like our forefathers did. This is the new sexual revolution. Like prohibition, time will pass and the government will realize that they were wrong "again." This is harmless. That would be another step to freeing America from the old laws made when homosexuality was not even considered natural. Things have changed, and if the government doesn't get with the system, then we should change the government. The world was confused. Sex lives being censored. The story continues.

Appendix B

"More of a Man" from the video *More of a Man* (All Worlds Video, 1990).
Lyrics by Jerry Douglas.
Music by Lee Ward.

I've always been different, outside the norm;
Exotic, hypnotic, but much too neurotic to ever conform.
Always more of a daughter and less of a son;
Poetic, pathetic, but never athletic–a bit overdone.
Always less of a fella and more of a freak;
Dramatic, erratic, oh God it's traumatic when you're born to be chic
(in short life was a bitch).
Since militants' morality offended my mentality,
And my originality distorted their reality,
My life became a messy masquerade (very messy).
Until I told society "go fuck your prudish piety"
And traded my anxiety for shameless notoriety
My life remained a silly-assed charade.
Until you face hostility with total visibility
You'll never know tranquility or real respectability.
So join the passing parade.
Come sing this sweet serenade.
I'm more of an asset than you ever thought.
And I'm more of a bargain than you have ever bought.
And I'm less of a danger than you have been taught.
But more of a challenge than you have ever fought.
I'm more of a treasure than you can conceive.
And I'm more of a triumph than you can achieve.
I'm your doctor, I'm your lawyer, you better, better believe.
I'm your son and I'm your daughter so don't be so naive.
Come on! Deject me, inspect me,

But don't you reject me.
Deflect me, neglect me,
But damn it you better respect me.
And folks, you can take it from me.
This incredible creature you see
Has the best of both worlds, yessiree.
I'm more of a woman than you'll ever have,
And more of a man than you'll ever be.

Appendix C

Gay male pornographic videos viewed:

Abducted
Absolutely Uncut
Afternooners
Against the Rules
Alleycats
All Tied Up
America's Sexiest Home Videos
AMG: The Fantasy Factory
Arcade
Argos: The Session
Backdrop
Bad Ass
Bad Break
Bait
Bat Dude (and Throbbin)
Beach Blanket Boner
Beef
Behind Closed Doors
Below the Belt
Best of the Superstars
Better Than Ever
Big as They Come
Big Bang
Big Delivery
Big Guns
Bigger than Huge
Bigger than Life
Bigger the Better, The
Biggest One I Ever Saw, The

Big Men on Campus
Big One, The
Big Ones, The
Biker's Liberty
Billboard
Black Alley
Black in Demand
Black Magic
Black Men in Uniform
Black Shafts
Black Sweat
Black Trade
Black Workout 3
Blow Your Own Horn
Bodymasters, The
Bondage Reunion
Boots and Saddles
Bore n Stroke
Born to Raise Hell
Boxer, The
Boxer 2, The
Boys in the Sand
Boys in the Sand II
Boys of El Barrio
Boys of Venice, The
Brawnzmen, The
Breaker Blue
Break In
Brief Encounters
Bronx Crew: Hooked on Hispanics 2
Brute
Buckshot-Minute Man Series 2
Buckshot-Minute Man Series 7: Rawhide Roundup
Buckshot-Minute Man Series 9
Buckshot-Minute Man Series 10
Buddy System
Buddy System II
Bulge: Mass Appeal

Busted
Cabin Fever
Caged Heat
Call of the Wild
Captured
Caribbean Beat
Carnaval in Rio
Carnival in Venice
Caught in the Act
Centurians of Rome
Century Mining
Chained Reactions
Cherry, The
Chicago Meat Packers
Chip Off the Old Block
C.H.P.
Classified Action
Closed Set
Closed Set II
Cocksure
Cocktales
Colt (volumes 1-12)
Come as You Are
Coming Soon
Command Performance
Company We Keep, The
Compulsion: He's Gotta Have It
Cop Luv
Corporate Head
Cousins Should Do It
Cowboys and Indians
Crosswire
Cruisin': Men on the Make
Cruisin' 2: More Men on the Make
Cult of Manhood
Cycle Studs
Daddy Bare
Daisy Chain Spanking

Dangerous
Davey and the Cruisers
Day in the Life, A
Deep in Hot Water
Deep Inside Jon Vincent
Delivery Boys
Desert Drifters
Destroying Angel
Diary, The
Dirt Busters
Dirty Dreaming
Dirty Tricks
Discharged
Disconnected
Doing It
Dorm Fever
Down Home
Down to His Knee
Dreamers
Drifters, The
Dude: Le Beau Mec
Dynastud
Easy Riders
Ebony Eagles
Eight Men In
El Paso Wrecking Corp.
Erotikus
Everhard
Every Which Way
Faces
Face to Face
Fade In
Falconhead
Falconhead II: The Maneaters
Fan Male
Fantasize
Fast Friends
Fast Idle (w/*The Photo Shoot* and *Fast Idle video*)

Few Good Men, A
Find This Man
Filth
First Mate
First Time, The
First Time Broken
Flashbacks
Flesh and Fantasy
Flexx
Forty Plus
4 Alarm Stud
Foxhole
Frank Vickers Volume II: Worship
Frank Vickers Volume III
Frathouse Memories
French Kiss
Full Length
Full Load
Full Service
Games
Gay Erotica from the Past #1
Gayracula
Getting It
Giants
Giant Splash Shots II
G.I. Mac
Gloryhole Video #1: Tom's Foreskin Obsession
Golden Boys of the SS
Gold Rush Boys
Good Hot Stuff
Grand Prize
Gridiron
Hard Knocks
Hard Steal
Hard to Believe
Hard to Come By
Hard to Hold
Hart Throb

Head of the Class
Heads or Tails
Head Struck
Head Trips
Healthy and Young Slaves in Training
Heat in the Night
Heat Stroke
Heavenly
Heavy Load
He-Devils
Hidden Camera
Hole in One
Honorable Jones
Horsemeat
Hotel Hell
Hot House
Hot, Hung, and Hard
Hot Lunch
Hot Male Mechanics
Hot Pursuit
Hot Rods: The Young and the Hung Part 2
Hot to Trot
Huge Double Impact
Huge Torpedoes
Hung and Dangerous
Idol Eyes
Idol Thoughts
Idol Worship
Inch by Inch
Inches
In Hot Pursuit
Inner Circle, The
Interracial Affairs
In the Grasp
In the Raw
Intruders
In Your Wildest Dreams
Island Fever

Island Heat
Job Site
Jumper
Just Between Us
Kansas City Trucking Co.
Keeping Time
Key West Bellhop
Kinky Stuff
King Size
Kiss Off
Knight Out With the Boys
Knockout
L.A. Plays Itself
L.A. Sex Stories
Las Vegas Love Gods
Latin Cop Sex
L.A. Tool and Die
Law and Order
Leather Me Down, Do Me Toys
Leather Report, The
Left-Handed
Legend of Mine 69, The
Leo and Lance
Lewd Conduct
Lifeguard
Lifeguard on Duty
Like a Horse
Like Moths to a Flame
Loaded
Long Hot Summer, The
Long John
Long Johns II
Look, The
Los Hombres
Lunch Hour
Made for You
Madness & Method
Main Attraction, The

Male Instinct
Male Taboo
Malibu Pool Boys
Mandriven
Manhattan Latin
Manly Beach
Mannequin Man
Man of the Year
Man Stroke
Master of the Discipline, The
Master Piece
Matter of Size, A
Mechanics on Duty
Members Only
Men and Steel
Men of the Midway
Men on Call
Men: Skin, and Steel
Men With No Name
Midnight Snack
Midnight Sun
Military Heat
Mocha Madness
More of a Man
Motorpunks
Motorsexual
Muscle Bound Men 2
Muscle Ranch
Muscle Up
My Cousin Danny
My Masters
Naked Lunch
Never Big Enough
New Breed, The
New Love
New Zealand Undercover
Next Valentino, The
Night Alone with Al Parker, A

Night at Halsted's, A
Night at the Adonis, A
Night Crawlers
Night Flight
Night Force
Nighthawks in Leather
Nights in Black Leather
Non-Stop
Northwest Passage
Object of Desire
Obsession
Obsession: Hot Rods of Steel
Old Reliable #72
One in a Billion
One, Two, Three
On the Lookout
On the Rocks
Open House
Other Side of Aspen, The
Other Side of Aspen II, The
Out of Bounds
Outpost
Outrage
Overload
Oversize Load
Pacific Coast Highway 2
Package Delivery
Palm Springs 92264
Palm Springs Paradise
Party Hard
Penetration
Perfect Summer
Pictures from the Black Dance
Piece of Cake
Pinball Wiz
Pink Narcissus
Pipeline
Pits, Tits, and Feet

Pizza Boy, He Delivers
Pleasure Beach
Pledgemasters, The
Plunge
Powerfull II
Power Play
Powertool
Powertool 2: Breaking Out
Private Dancer
Private, the D.I., and the Lover, The
Private Workout
Producer, The
Pumping Up: Flexx II
Queer: The Movie
Raising Hell
Ram Man 2
Ranch Hand
Ranger Nick
Rangers
Raunch
Raunch II
Rawhide
Razor's Edge
Real Men of the New West
Recaptured
Red Ball Express
Redwood Ranger
Revenge: More Than I Can Take
Revenge of the Nighthawk
Right Here, Right Now
Rimshot
Rip Colt's Sex-Rated Home Movies
Rise, The
Rites of Fall
River, The
Rock Hard
Rod Squad, The
Route 69

Running Hard
Sailor in Sydney, A
Sailor in the Wild
Sailor in the Wild II
Salsa Fever
Santa Monica Boulevard
Say Goodbye
School Daze
Scent of Man, A
Scorcher
Score Ten
Scoring
Scott Answer's Spring Break Bondage Boys
Screen Play
Sex Behind Bars
Sex Drive 2020
Sex Garage
Sex in Tight Places
Sex in Wet Places
Sex, Lies, and Video Cassettes
Sex Magic
Sexpress
Sex School
Sex Shooters
Sex Shooters II
Sexy Billy Blue
Sgt. Swann's Private File
Shadows in the Night
Shaft, The
Shake That Thing
Shoot
Shore Leave
Sighs
Single White Male
Sizing Up
Skin Deep
Skin Torpedoes
Slaves for Sale

Slave's Submission
Slave Workshop - Hamburg
Slave Workshop - L. A.
Some Men are Bigger than Others
Someone is Watching
Songs in the Key of Sex
Soul and Salsa
Soul and Salsa II
Soul Dad
Spank
Splash Shots
Splash Tops
Spokes
Spokes II: The Graduation
Spread Eagle
Spring Break
Spring Semester
Spring Training
Steel Dungeon
Steel Garters
Sterling Ranch
Sticky Gloves
Straight Pick-up 2
Straight Studs
Stranded: Enemies and Lovers
Street Kids
Stroke, The
Stryker Force
Stud Busters
Stud Struck
Summer Buddies
Superhunk
Take Down
Tattoo
Tattoo Love Boy
Tease Me
That Boy
These Bases Are Loaded

They Grow 'em Big
Thinking Big
Three Day Pass
Three Little Pigs
Toilets
Tony's Initiation
Tool of the Trade
To the Bone
Touch Me
Tough
Tough and Tender
Tough Competition
Tough, Hungry Men
Trade-Off
Tramps
Trash
Trilogy
Tropical Heatwave
True Confessions
Turned On
1230 West Melrose
Two by Ten
Two Handfuls
Two Handfuls Part II
Uncut Club of Los Angeles
Undercover
Under the Sign of the Stallion
Unfriendly Persuasion
Uniformed Fantasy
Uniformed Fantasy II
Uninhibited and Uncut
USSM/One
USSM/Four
View to a Thrill
View to a Thrill II: The Man with the Golden Rod
Visitor, The
Voyeur
Wanted

Wanted: Billy the Kid
Warlords
Water Works
Weekend at Large
Weekend Lockup
Wet
What the Big Boys Eat
White on White
White Steel
Wide Load
Wild and Loose
Wild Obsession
Wild Streak
Willing to Take It
Windows
Winner's Way
Winner Takes All
Working Stiffs
Zeusman 2

References

Bersani, Leo. 1987. "Is the Rectum a Grave?" *October*, Issue 43, pp. 197-222.

Brantley, Doug. 1993. "Joe Blow." *The Advocate*, 23 March, p. 79.

Bright, Susie. 1990. "How to Read a Dirty Movie." Paper presented at Collective For Living Cinema, 1 November, New York, NY.

Bronski, Michael. 1984. *Culture Clash: The Making of Gay Sensibility*. Boston: South End Press.

Califia, Pat. 1988. "Among Us, Against Us: The New Puritans." In *Caught Looking: Feminism, Pornography & Censorship*, edited by Kate Ellis, Beth Jaker, Nan D. Hunter, Barbara O'Dair, and Abby Tallmer. Seattle: The Real Comet Press, pgs. 20-25.

Chapman, David. 1989. *Adonis: The Male Physique Pin-Up 1870-1940*. London: GMP Publishers.

Charles, Sidney. 1976. Review of *Born to Raise Hell*. *Drummer*, January/February, p. 15

Colby, Cord, Dennis Walsh, and Jack Wrangler. 1991. "Lights! Camera! Action!" Panel Discussion at the Glines Theatre, 19 May, New York, NY.

Crimp, Douglas. 1987. "How to Have Promiscuity in an Epidemic." In *AIDS: Cultural Analysis, Cultural Activism*, edited by Douglas Crimp. Cambridge: MIT Press, pgs. 237-271.

Douglas, Jerry. 1992. "The Legend of Casey Donovan." *Manshots*, April, pp. 67-73.

Dyer, Richard. 1990. *Now You See It: Studies on Lesbian and Gay Film*. New York: Routledge.

Dyer, Richard. 1985. "Male Gay Porn: Coming to Terms." *Jump Cut*, n.d., Issue 30, pp. 27-29.

Finch, Mark. 1989. "Rio Limpo: 'Lonesome Cowboys' and Gay Cinema." In *Andy Warhol: Film Factory*, edited by Michael O'Pray. London: British Film Institute, pgs. 112-117.

Fung, Richard. 1991. "Looking For My Penis: The Eroticized Asian in Gay Video Porn." In *How Do I Look?* edited by Bad Object-Choices. Seattle: Bay Press, pgs. 145-168.

Idol, Ryan. 1991. Interview by David Kalmansohn. *Frontiers*, 15 February, pp. 39-44.

Kalin, Tom 1992. "Flesh Histories." In *A Leap in the Dark: AIDS, Art & Contemporary Cultures*, edited by Allan Klusacek and Ken Morrison. Montreal: Vehicule Press, pgs. 120-135.

Kendrick, Walter. 1987. *The Secret Museum*. New York: Penguin Books.

Koch, Gertrude. 1990. "The Body's Shadow Realm: On Pornographic Cinema." *Jump Cut*, n.d., No. 35, pp. 17-29.

Levi Kamel, G.W. 1983. "The Leather Career: On Becoming a Sadomasochist." In *S and M: Studies in Sadomasochism*, edited by Thomas Weinberg and G. W. Levi Kamel. Buffalo: Prometheus Books, pgs. 73-79.

Leyland, Winston. 1982. *Physique: A Pictorial History of the Athletic Model Guild*. San Francisco: Gay Sunshine Press.

Mains, Geoff. 1984. *Urban Aboriginals: A Celebration of Leathersexuality*. San Francisco: Gay Sunshine Press.

Olson, David. 1991. "Film Seized in Police Raid at Bijou Theatre." *Windy City Times*, 21 February, pp. 1, 18,47.

Parker, Al. 1990. Interview with author. 12 March, Los Angeles, CA.

Patton, Cindy. 1991. "Safe Sex and the Pornographic Vernacular." In *How Do I Look?* edited by Bad Object-Choices. Seattle: Bay Press, pgs. 31-64.

Poole, Wakefield. 1972. Interview by Robert Colaciello. *Interview*, May, p. 22.

Popular Memory Group. 1982. "Popular Memory: Theory, Politics, Method." In *Making Histories*, edited by Johnson and McLennan. Minneapolis: University of Minnesota Press, pgs. 205-252.

Pronger, Brian. 1990. *The Arena of Masculinity: Sports, Homosexuality, and the Meaning of Sex*. New York: St. Martin's Press.

Purusha. 1981. *The Divine Androgyne: Adventures in Cosmic Erotic Ecstasy and Androgyne Bodyconsciousness*. San Diego: Sanctuary Publications.

Rowberry, John. 1993. *The Adam Film World 1993 Handbook: Gay Adult Video.* Los Angeles: Knight Publishing.

Rowberry, John. 1992. *The Adam Film World 1992 Handbook: Gay Adult Video.* Los Angeles: Knight Publishing.

Rowberry, John. 1991. *The Adam Film World 1992 Directory: Gay Adult Video.* Los Angeles: Knight Publishing.

Rowberry, John. 1990. *The Adam Film World 1991 Directory: Gay Adult Video.* Los Angeles: Knight Publishing.

Rowberry, John. 1986. *Gay Video: A Guide to Erotica.* San Francisco: G.S. Press.

Siebenand, Paul. 1975. "The Beginnings of Gay Cinema In Los Angeles: The Industry and the Audience." PhD dissertation, University of Southern California.

Slater, J.D. 1990. Interview by Rick Grzesiak. *Edge*, 5 December, pp. 25-31.

Stoltenberg, John. 1990. "Gays and the Propornography Movement: Having the Hots for Sex Discrimination." In *Men Confront Pornography*, edited by Michael S. Kimmel. New York: Crown Publishers, pgs. 248-262.

Stryker, Jeff. 1990. Interview by David Rimanelli. *Interview*, December, pp. 134-141.

Styles, Joseph. 1979. "Outsider/Insider: Researching Gay Baths." *Urban Life*, July, pp. 135-152.

Townsend, Larry. 1983. *The Leatherman's Handbook II.* New York: Carlyle Communications.

Travis, John and Matt Sterling. 1989. Interview by Kevin Koffler. *The Advocate*, 12 September, pp. 29-30.

Turan, Kenneth and Stephen F. Zito. 1974. *Sinema: American Pornographic Films and the People Who Make Them.* New York: Praeger Publishers.

Wall, F. 1992. "Live and On Location: Making a Porn Flick." *The Guide*, November, pp. 16-20.

Waugh, Tom. 1992. "Homoerotic Representation in the Stag Film 1920-1940: Imagining an Audience." *Wide Angle*, n.d., Vol. 14, No. 2, pp. 4-19.

Waugh, Tom. 1985. "Men's Pornography: Gay vs. Straight." *Jump Cut*, n.d., Issue 30, pp. 30-35.

Williams, Linda. 1989. *Hardcore: Power, Pleasure, and the "Frenzy of the Visible."* Berkeley: University of California Press.
Wockner, Rex. 1991. "Major Obscenity Case on Deck in Chicago." *Outline*, March, p. 21.
Wrangler, Jack and Carl Johnes. 1984. *The Jack Wrangler Story.* New York: St. Martin's Press.
Young, David. 1991. Interview with author. 16 February, New York, NY.

Suggested Reading

Aletti, Vince. 1992. "Boys on Film." *The Village Voice*, 11 August, p. 95.

Arcand, Bernard. 1992. "Erotica and Behaviour Change: The Anthropologist as Voyeur." In *A Leap in the Dark: AIDS, Art & Contemporary Cultures*, edited by Allan Klusacek and Ken Morrison. Montreal: Vehicule Press, pgs. 173-176.

Attorney General's Commission on Pornography. 1986. *Final Report*. Washington, DC: U.S. Government Printing Office.

Babbitt, Dave. 1992. "Glory Holes in Gay Film Erotica." *Manshots*, April, pp. 10-17.

Berlin, Peter. 1991. Part I of a two-part interview by Bruce La-Bruce. *J.D.s*, n.d. No. 7, pp. 39-46.

Berlin, Peter. 1991. Part II of interview by Bruce LaBruce. *J.D.s*, n.d., No. 8, pp. 35-42.

Bull, Chris. 1990. "New York's Peter Staley: Activism as the Best Therapy," *The Advocate*, 13 February, n.p.

Burger, John R. 1992. "Laying the Saints: Toward the Queer Canonization of Gay Male Porn Stars Dead From AIDS." Paper presented at symposium, *Explicit Sex: Art or Phallacy*, 24 January, at New York University, New York, NY.

Carlomusto, Jean and Gregg Bordowitz. 1989. "Do It! Safer Sex Porn for Girls and Boys Comes of Age." *Outweek*, 28 August, pp. 38-41.

Carter, Angela. 1978. *The Sadeian Woman and the Ideology of Pornography*. New York: Pantheon Books.

Chandler, Rex. 1992. Interview by Sabin. *GV Guide*, February, pp. 52-55.

Chapman, David. 1991. *Mountain Men: The Male Photography of Don Whitman*. London: GMP Publishers.

Charles, Sidney. 1976. Review of Michael Zen's *Falconhead*. *Drummer*, July, pp. 60-61.

Chicago Hellfire Club. 1986. *Inferno XV Runbook*. San Francisco: Desmodus.

Cibellis, Matthew. 1993. "Kiss My Foot: Bob Jones" DIY Fetish Film Empire." *New York Press*, 28 July-3 August, pp. 18-21.

Clark, Chris. 1990. "Pornography Without Power?" In *Men Confront Pornography*, edited by Michael S. Kimmel. New York: Crown Publishers.

Corbin, Jake. 1991. "The Two Jakes." *Hunt*, n.d., Issue 33, pp. 8-10.

Dallesandro, Joe. 1984. Interview by Jim Yousling. *In Touch*, March, pp. 60-66.

DeGenevieve, Barbara. 1991. "Masculinity and its Discontents." *SF Camerawork*, Summer/Fall, pp. 3-12.

DeStefano, George. 1990. "A Wank Through History." *Outweek*, 9 May, pp. 38-42.

Duncan, Philip. 1969. "Lights . . . Action . . . Camera–Roll It, Mary!" *Queen's Quarterly*, Fall, pp. 32-33, 45.

Ellenzweig, Allen. 1992. *The Homoerotic Photograph*. New York: Columbia University Press.

Elliott, Harvey. 1978. "Cultivating the Avant-Garden." *After Dark*, May, p. 52.

Fleming, Charles. 1991. "Adult Video Producers Organize for Free Speech and a New Image." *The Advocate*, 16 July, p. 52.

Foster, Alasdair. 1988. *Behold the Man: The Male Nude in Photography*. Edinburgh: Stills Gallery.

Foucault, Michel. 1978. *The History of Sexuality: An Introduction* New York: Vintage Books.

Fritscher, Jack. 1977. "Pumping Roger: Acts, Facts, & Fantasy." *Drummer*, n.d., Issue 21, pp. 45-46, 68.

Giles, Jane. 1991. *The Cinema of Jean Genet*. London: BFI Publishing.

Greenberg, David F. 1988. *The Construction of Homosexuality*. Chicago: University of Chicago Press.

Greyson, John. 1992. "A Kiss is Not a Kiss." *Afterimage*, January, pp. 10-13.

Gunther, Matt. 1992. Interview by Sabin. *Gay Video Guide*, December, pp. 32-35, 46-47.

Halsted, Fred. 1972. Interview by Ernest Peter Cohen. *Gay Activist*, April, pp. 11, 21-22.

Huber, Ted. 1989. "Scenarios Set in the Fires of Hell: *Inferno The Motion Picture.*" *Drummer*, December, pp. 11-16.

Idol, Ryan. 1992. Interview by Sabin. *Gay Video Guide*, August, pp. 32-35, 48.

Ischar, Doug. 1990. "Endangered Alibis." *Afterimage*, May, pp. 8-11.

Kearns, Michael. 1980. "The Gage Boys are Rolling Again with *L.A. Tool & Die.*" *Drummer*, n.d., Issue 34, pp. 20-22.

Kinnick, Dave. 1993. *Sorry I Asked: Intimate Interviews with Gay Porn's Rank and File*. New York: Badboy.

Kinnick, Dave. 1991. "Big Boys, Big Secrets." *The Advocate*, 12 March, pp. 56-58.

Kinnick, Dave. 1991. "Putting His Best Foot Forward: Video Maker Bob Jones Brings His Fetish Out of the Closet and Onto the Screen." *The Advocate*, 18 June, p. 55.

Kinnick, Dave. 1991. "The Lust Weekend: Diary Entries From a Pornographic Retreat, or How I Spent My Summer Vacation." *The Advocate*, 24 September, pp. 78-79.

Kinnick, Dave. 1991. "Lights! Camera! Condoms!: How Safe is Video Sex?" *Frontiers*, 27 September, pp. 45-50.

Kinnick, Dave. 1991. "Travels in Porn America: Touring the United States Via Gay Videos." *The Advocate 1991 Travel America Guide*, pp. 20-21.

Levi Kamel, G.W. 1983. "Leathersex: Meaningful Aspects of Gay Sadomasochism." In *S and M: Studies in Sadomasochism*, edited by Thomas Weinberg and G. W. Levi Kamel. Buffalo: Prometheus Books, pgs. 162-174.

Locke, Richard. 1987. *In the Heat of Passion: How to Have Hotter, Safer Sex*. San Francisco: Leyland Publications.

Locke, Richard. 1978. Interview by Eric Van Meter. *Drummer*, n.d., Issue 24, pp. 28-30, 74-75.

Mercer, Kobena. 1991. "Skin Head Sex Thing: Racial Difference and the Homoerotic Imaginary." In *How Do I Look?* edited by Bad Object-Choices. Seattle: Bay Press, pgs. 169-222.

Mohr, Richard D. 1992. *Gay Ideas: Outing and Other Controversies*. Boston: Beacon Press.

Nichols, Bill. 1981. *Ideology and the Image.* Bloomington: Indiana University Press.

Patrick, John. 1992. *The Best of the Superstars 1993: The Year in Sex.* Sarasota: STARbooks Press.

Patrick, John. 1992. *The Best of the Superstars 1992: The Year in Sex.* Sarasota: STARbooks Press.

Patrick, John. 1991. *The Best of the Superstars 1991: The Year in Sex.* Sarasota: STARbooks Press.

Patrick, John. 1991. *Legends: The World's Sexiest Men Volume One.* Sarasota: STARbooks Press.

Patrick, John. 1991. *Lowe Down: Tim Lowe.* Sarasota: STARbooks Press.

Patrick, John. 1990. *A Charmed Life: Vince Cobretti.* Sarasota: STARbooks Press.

Patrick, John. 1989. *The Best of the Superstars.* Tampa: STARbooks Press.

Patton, Cindy. 1992. "Designing Safer Sex: Pornography as Vernacular." In *A Leap in the Dark: AIDS, Art & Contemporary Cultures,* edited by Allan Klusacek and Ken Morrison. Montreal: Vehicule Press, pgs. 192-206.

Pendleton, David. 1992. "Obscene Allegories: Narrative, Representation, Pornography." *Discourse,* Fall, pp. 154-168.

Poole, Wakefield. 1978. Interview by Jack Fritscher. *Drummer,* n.d., Issue 27, pp. 14-22.

Preston, John and Glenn Swann. 1986. *Safe Sex: The Ultimate Erotic Guide.* New York: Plume.

Rage, Christopher. 1990. Interview by J.D. Slater. *Drummer,* September, pp. 7-10.

Reyes, Nina. 1990. "Smothering Smut." *Outweek,* 26 September, pp. 37-42.

Ross, Andrew. 1989. *No Respect: Intellectuals and Popular Culture.* New York: Routledge.

Rutledge, Leigh W. 1989. *The Gay Fireside Companion.* Boston: Alyson Publications.

Scarry, Elaine. 1985. *The Body in Pain.* New York: Oxford University Press.

Seipp, Catherine. 1992. "Beauty and the Butt." *The Advocate,* n.d., pp. 52-53.

Serafini, James. 1992. "The Masculine Mystique." *QW*, 9 August, p. 48.

Sikes, Neal. 1975. "Devautee of Porn." *The Soho Weekly News*, 13 November, n.p.

Simmons, Joe. 1991. Interview by Allen Bell. *BLK*, June, pp. 6-16.

Sommers, Danny. 1992. Interview by Robert W. Richards. *Manshots*, April, pp. 53-59.

Speck, Wieland. 1992. "Working with the Film Language of Porn: A German View of Safer Sex." In *A Leap in the Dark: AIDS, Art & Contemporary Cultures*, edited by Allan Klusacek and Ken Morrison. Montreal: Vehicule Press, pgs. 184-191.

Stefano, Joey. 1991. Interview by Sabin. *GV Guide*, Summer, pp. 20-25.

Stoltenberg, John. 1990. "Pornography and Freedom." In *Men Confront Pornography*, edited by Michael S. Kimmel. New York: Crown publishers, pgs. 60-71.

Stoltenberg, John. 1990. *Refusing to Be a Man: Essays on Sex and Justice*. New York: Meridian.

Stryker, Jeff. 1991. Interview by Sabin. *GV Guide*, Fall, pp. 52-57.

Stryker, Jeff. 1989. Interview by Kevin Koffler. *The Advocate*, 12 September pp. 26-30.

Taylor, Scott. 1991. *Danse Macabre, A Dark Ride: Autobiographical Programme & Tribute to Photographers*. San Francisco: Little Black Books.

Thomas, Karl. 1992. Interview by William Spencer. *Manshots*, April, pp. 27-31.

Thompson, Michael. 1991. "A Porn Star is Born!" *The Guide*, November, pp. 112-115.

Timmons, Stuart. 1992. "Wanted: Athletic Models." *The Advocate*, 30 July, pp. 56-60.

Touraine, Alain. 1988. *Return of the Actor*. Minneapolis: University of Minnesota Press.

Townsend, Larry. 1992. "Hot Men in the Wild." *Drummer*, March, pp. 23-26.

Trecker, Barbara. 1974. "Porn's Two Male Superstars." *New York Post*, 21 November, n.p.

Tucker, Scott. 1990. "Gender, Fucking, and Utopia: An Essay in

Response to John Stoltenberg's *Refusing to Be a Man.*" *Social Text*, No. 27, pp. 3-34.

Tucker, Scott. 1990. "Radical Feminism and Gay Male Porn." In *Men Confront Pornography*, edited by Michael S. Kimmel. New York: Crown Publishers, pgs. 263-276.

Tyler, Parker. 1972. *Screening the Sexes: Homosexuality in the Movies.* New York: Holt, Rinehart and Winston.

Umlaut, John. 1989. "Fright, Cameras, Action!" *Outweek*, 28 August, pp. 35-37, 80.

Walker, Christian. 1991. "The Miscegenated Gaze." *SF Camerawork*, Summer/Fall, pp. 13-20.

Walters, Margaret. 1978. *The Nude Male: A New Perspective.* New York: Paddington Press.

Watney, Simon. 1987. *Policing Desire: Pornography, AIDS and the Media.* Minneapolis: University of Minnesota Press.

Waugh, Tom. 1992. "Erotic Self-Images in the Gay Male AIDS Melodrama." In *Fluid Exchanges: Artists and Critics in the AIDS Crisis*, edited by James Miller. Toronto: University of Toronto Press.

Waugh, Tom. 1984. "Photography Passion & Power." *The Body Politic*, March, pp. 29-33.

Waugh, Tom. 1983. "A Heritage of Pornography." *The Body Politic*, January, pp. 29-33.

Webster, Paula. 1988. "Pornography and Pleasure." In *Caught Looking: Feminism, Pornography & Censorship*, edited by Kate Ellis, Beth Jaker, Nan D. Hunter, Barbara O'Dair, and Abby Tallmer. Seattle: The Real Comet Press, pgs. 30-35.

Wrangler, Jack. 1976. Interview. *Drummer*, July, pp. 4-6.

Index

Abstinence, as safe sex, 30
Acquired immune deficiency
    syndrome, (AIDS),
    22-24,27,28,30,31,46,
    78,80,81
  fundraising for, 82
  politicization of, 31
ACT UP, 27,28,31,82,86
Adam Film World 1991 Directory,
    The, 38,53-54,55
Adam Film World 1992 Directory,
    The, 12-13
  description of, 13*n.*
Adonis, The (New York), 44
Adult Video News Awards (1990),
    96,96*n.,* 98
Advertising, of Calvin Klein
    Underwear, 25-26
Advocate, The, 14,73,81
Al Parker's Sexiest Home Videos, 46
Altman, Robert, 35,90
American Cream, 18
Amyl Nitrite. *See* Poppers
Androgyne, definition of, 61
Andy Warhol's Dracula, 12
Andy Warhol's Frankenstein, 12
Anger, Kenneth, 9,14,15
Ardent, Keith, 86
Arena (Los Angeles), 82
Arena of Masculinity, The, 102
Ashfield, David, 76
Asian Knights, 57
Ast, Pat, 12
Athletic Model Guild (AMG),
    7-8,9,14,15
  and Hollywood epics, 8
  vice raid of, 8
Aztec Sacrifice, 8

Baldwin, Lex, 28,74,80
Bat Dude, 73
Bathhouses, 34,43,43*n.,* 46
Beers, Robert, 19*n.*
Bellas, Bruce. *See* Bruce
    of Los Angeles
Below The Belt, 56,57
Berlin, Peter, 19
Bersani, Leo, 40-41
Berube, Allan, 33
Better Than Ever, 47
BIC Productions, 80
Bigger the Better, The, 23
Bijou Theater
  lawsuit against, 97
  vice sweep of, 96
Black Attack, 55
Black Shafts, 54
Black Sweat, 54
"Bloopers." *See Screwing Screw
    Ups*
Blow Your Own Horn, 30
Blue Movie (aka *Fuck*), 10-11
Bond, Scott, 80
Born to Raise Hell, 16,17-18,19,63
Boys in the Sand, 16,18,45
Boys of El Barrio, 54
Brando, Marlon, 36
Brantley, Doug, 14
Bright, Susie, 73
Brinks robbery, 72
Brock, Tom, 25
Bronski, Michael, 85
Bruce of Los Angeles, 8,9,11
Buckshot, 30
Burns, Chris, 59,82-83

Burton, Joseph, 97
Busted, 87-88
Buster, 23

Cadinot, Jean-Daniel, 35
Califia, Pat, 101
Catalina Video, 80
Cage, John, and the *I Ching*, 64
Caligula, 34
Call Off Your Old Tired Ethics
    (COYOTE), 48
Canby, Vincent, 16
Carnival in Venice, 35
Centurians of Rome, 35
    financing of, 72
Chandler, Rex, 28,74
Chant D'Amour, Un, 9
    banning of, 9
Chapman, David, 6
Charles, Sidney, 18
Chauncey, George Jr., 33
Chicago Police Department Vice
    Control, 97
Chip Off the Old Block, 54,58
Christopher, John, 35
Close-ups, 76
Club Baths (San Francisco), 43
Cocteau, Jean, 14
Coe, Clinton, 23
Colby, Cord, 55
Colored Boys, 54,55
Colt Studio, 24,30,82
Coming Out Under Fire, 33,37
Commission on Pornography and
    Obscenity, The, 14
Condoms, 27,28
Conners, Dave, 27
Coppola, Francis Ford, 12
Corbin, Jake, 82,83
Coronet Theater (Los Angeles), 9
Cotton Club, The, 12
Couch, 9,10
Cowboys and Indians, 35
Crimp, Douglas, 31-32

Cruisin' '57, 36
Cry Baby, 12
"cum shot," 29,76-78
Cycle Studs, 15

Daguerre, Louis, 6
Dallesandro, Joe, 11
    career of, 11-14
Damien, 30
Davey and the Cruisers, 36
Davis, Tamra, 12
Days of the Greek Gods, The, 9
Dcota, 76
Dennis, Patrick, 36
Design Industries Foundation for
    AIDS (DIFFA), 82
Desire, homosexual, 40
Destroying Angel, 18
DeVeau, Jack, 12,13,19,44,71
Diary, The, 15
Divine Androgyne, The, 61
Dominant Memory
    definition of, 2
    inequities of, 59
    and racism, 57
Donovan, Casey, 16,23,25,45,72
Donovan, Rick, 25,92
Doubles, for porn stars, 76
Douglas, Jerry, 16,95,96
Drummer, 15,18
Duberman, Martin, 33
Dungeons of Europe, 63
Dyer, Richard, 10,15,17,18,21-22,27

Earl, Roger, 16,17-18,63
Ebony Eagles, 54
Edge, 80,81
Eliot, Josh, 87
El Paso Wrecking Corp., 40,58,59
*Exclusive Sailor, The. See La
    Maitresse Du Capitaine De
    Meydeux*

Factory, The, 11
Falconhead, 18

Falcon Studios, 45
Fanon, Frantz, 56
Fatale, Fanny, 101
Federal Bureau of Investigations
    (FBI), 87
Feminists Fighting Pornography, 101
55th Street Playhouse (New York),
    16
Finch, Mark, 10
Fire Island, 45
Fireworks, 9,10
First Amendment, The, 97
Fistfucking, 19*n*.
Flaming Creatures, 9,10,15
    banning of, 10
Flesh, 11
Flexx, Lonn, 93
Fluffers, 75-76
Fontaine, Richard, 8-9
40 Plus, 54,57,58
Foster, Cody, 80
Foxhole, 36
Frontiers, 76,81
Fung, Richard, 56-57

Gage, Joe, 40,72,75,77
Galdi, Vincenzo, 6
Gay environments, 46
Gay invisibility, 39,41
Gay liberation, 31
    movement, 14
    and pornography, 3
Gay Men's Health Crisis (GMHC),
    31,86
Gay pride, 11,28
Gayracula, 89
Gay rights, 14
Gender roles
    ideologies of, 102
    as myth, 39,41
Genet, Jean, 9,15
Glover, Kevin, 47
Gold Rush Boys, 35
Grease, 36

Greece, ancient, 5
Greenwich Village piers, 43,44,44*n*.
GunCrazy, 12
Gunther, Matt, 50

Halsted, Fred, 16,17,18,19*n*., 44,58
Hammond, Steve, 50
Hardcore, 77
Heat, 12
Heatstroke, 23,58,72,75,77
Henson, Michael, 91
Heterosexism, 21
Heterosexual identity, violation
    of, 41
Heterosexual stereotypes, gay men's
    identification with, 41
Hidden Camera, 64
Hidden From History, 33,37
Hill, Lonnie, 96
Hin Yin For Men, 30
Historiography, standards of, 33
History
    gay and lesbian, 33
    and historicization, 2
    political relevance of, 42
    production of gay male, 3
History-writing, 33
HIV transmission, 27,29
Homeboy Workout, 54
Homoerotic art, censorship of, 6
Homoeroticism, in advertising, 26
Homophobia, 25
    in advertising, 26
Hompertz, Tom, 11
Honorable Jones, 15
Horse Hung Hispanics, 54,55
Hot House, 12,71

Idol Eyes, 76
Idol, Ryan, 74,76,82
Inauguration of the Pleasuredome,
    15
In Hot Pursuit, 35
International Skin, 56

Interview, 25,50
In the Heat of Passion, 82
I, Rick, 65

Janssen, Volker, 11
Jeffries, Frank, 35
Johnes, Carl, 71
Johnson, Lyndon, 14
Johnson, Thor, 54
Jones, Bob, 64
Jump Cut, 53
Jumper, 88

Kalin, Tom, 25-26
Kansas City Trucking Co., 40,58
Kendall, Bobby, 16
Kendrick, Walter, 14
King, Rodney, 63
Klein, Calvin, underwear
     advertising, 25-26
Knight Out with the Boys, 69-70
Koch, Gertrude, 37
Kramer, Larry, 31

LaBruce, Bruce, 90
L.A. Plays Itself, 16,17,19
Larking, Peter. *See* Purusha
LaRue, Chi Chi, 73*n*, 91,96
L.A. Tool & Die, 23-24,40,58
Law and Order, 86-87
Leatherman's Handbook II, The, 60
Leave it to Beaver, 36
Lebowitz, Fran, 82
Left-Handed, 19
Levi Kamel, G. W., 67
Leyland, Winston, 11
Lifeguard, 27
Like Moths to a Flame, 62,63
Literature, gay and lesbian, 33-34
Live Video, 64
Lloyds of London, 72*n*.
Locke, Richard, 24,58,82

Lonesome Cowboys, 9,10,11,13
Long John, 15
Love Ball, 2,82
Loves of Ondine, The, 11
Lowe, Tim, 25
Ludlam, Charles, 15
Lunch Hour, 32

Madness & Method, 69-70,75,76,83
Mains, Geoff, 60
*Maitresse Du Capitaine De Meydeux
     La*, 7
Male bonding, 26
Man's Country Baths (New York),
     44*n*.
Marginalization, of gay community,
     1,2,46,102
Markopoulos, Gregory, 10,15
Mars (New York), 74
Marvin, Lee, 36
Marx, Karl, 33
Masculinity, 41
Master of the Discipline, The, 73
Masturbation, 30
Matthews, Ted, 48
Maxon, Brian, 25
McKenzie, Chris, 93
Memory, construction of, 3
Men Against Pornography (MAP),
     101
*Menage Moderne Du Madame
     Butterfly, Le*, 7
Men of the Midway, 59
Men with No Name, 63
Meriwether, Lewis, 35
Michelangelo's *David*, 6
Midnight Snack, 86,87
Miles, Sylvia, 12
Minute Man Video Series, 30
Mitchell, Thomas, 30
Mizer, Bob, 7-8,11,14
Models, fashion, 26
"Money shot." *See* "Cum shot"
More of a Man, 90
     and Catholicism, 95

and condom application, 94
and the deconstruction of
    masculinity, 95
and the gay rights movement, 94
plot synopsis of, 90-94
and political symbolism, 91,93,95
politics of, 95-97
as popular memory, 96
and racial integration, 96
and realism, 94
as revisionist pornography, 96
and safe sex, 97
the song, 93,95
Morgan, Robin, 78
Morgan, Scott, 54,57
Morrissey, Paul, 11,13
Motorpunks, 90
Motorsexual, 79
Museum of Modern Art (New York),
    19, 19*n.*
Musto, Michael, 74
Muybridge, Eadweard, and
    sequential action image
    studies, 7
My Thai Guy, 54

Nevels, Earl, 97
New Love, 46
New Right, 31
New York Jacks, 75
New York Times, The, 16
Next Valentino, The, 47,48,83
Night at Halsted's, A, 23,44
Night at the Adonis, A, 44
Nightclubs, backrooms in, 43*n.*
Nights in Black Leather, 18
Nixon, Richard, 14
Non-Stop, 44-45
Northern Lights Alternatives, 82
Northwest Passage, 35,42
No Skin Off My Ass, 90

Objectification, 76
Object of Desire, 87

Obscenity laws, 8
    in California, 18
    in Illinois, 97
Obscenity trials, 9-10
Oklahoma, and mail-order
    pornography, 37
Olson, David, 97
Old Reliable, 64-65,66
Ondine, 11
One in a Billion, 38
On the Rocks, 28-29,47,49-51
Oriental Dick, 54
Other Side of Aspen I, The, 45
Other Side of Aspen II, The, 45
Outrage, 73
Outweek, 74

Palm Drive Video, 65-66,70
Paris Theatre (Los Angeles), 16
Parker, Al, 24,25,34,46,75,80-81
Parks, Michael, 90-91
Park Theater (Los Angeles), 14
"Passing," 39
Patton, Cindy, 78
Payne, George, 35
Pearson, Ron, 45
Peckinpah, Sam, 35
Penraat, Jaap, 19
Pereyra, Michael, 82
Photography, and the male nude, 6
Physique films, 8
    and fetishism, 8
    and Greek mythology, 9
    history of, 8-9
    and the law, 8
Physique Pictorial, 8
Physique photography, 6-8,11,13
    censorship of, 6
    history of, 6-8
    purpose of, 6
Piccolo Pete, 7
Pictures from the Black Dance, 63
Pink Narcissus, 15-16,39
    and camp, 16
    Vincent Canby's review of, 16

Pines, The. *See* Fire Island
Pompeii, 5
Poole, Wakefield, 16
Poppers, 79*n*.
  use of in gay video pornography,
    79
Popular memory
  construction of, 83
  definition of, 2
  gay male, 21
  as political practice, 99
  and racism, 57
  and its role in society, 104
  study of, 53
Popular Memory Group, 2,33,
    34,38,85,99,104
  and popular struggles, 42,51,
    53,59,94
  and production of history, 3
"Pornlore," 50-51
  definition of, 49-50
"Pornographic Man, The", 73
Pornography, gay male
  history of, 3,5,7-8,13
Pornography, gay male video
  advertising of, 57,65-66
  and African-American men, 56
  and ageism, 54,57-59
  and AIDS, 22-24,27-28,
    30,78,79-80,83
  amateur, 46
  and anti-gay violence, 48-49,88
  and Asian men, 56-57
  and athleticism, 40
  and its audience, 51
  as autobiography, 46
  and auto-erotica, 29,30-31
  and bathhouses, 43-44
  as big business, 24
  and condom application, 29,32,78
  consumers' relation to titles of, 89
  and costuming, 39
  and cruising, 44-45

as cultural document, 4,5,21,26,
    32,34,43,44,45-46,47,48,49,
    50,51,53,54,57,59,67,83,86,99
  and the "daddy" type, 54
  and the deconstruction of
    masculinity, 40-41
  editing of, 5,28
  as erotic tool, 5
  and exhibitionism, 30,46
  as exhortations, 42
  and fantasy, 5,37
  and the FBI, 87-88
  and Fire Island, 45
  first release of, 15
  and gay bars, 44
  and gay environments, 43-46
  and the Gay Games, 43
  and gay male representation, 33
  and gay resorts, 45
  and gay rights, 86
  and gay visibility, 4,41,85-86
  and gender roles, 73,102
  and the Greenwich Village piers,
    43,44-45
  and heterosexuality, 24-26
  and heterosexual stereotypes,
    38-40,41,100
  and Hispanic men, 56
  history of, 14-19
  as history-writing, 21,33-42,
    51,83,99,104
  and homophobia, 26,88
  and homosocial environments,
    36,38-41
  industry, 69,73-74,78
    and off-set conditions, 81,82
    and its response to AIDS, 79-82
  as interactive agent, 51,83
  and internalized homophobia,
    58,102,105
  interracial, 55,87
  and the kinesthetics of sex, 5
  and looks-ism, 53,57
  mail-order market for, 37
  and masturbation, 30,31

and media technology, 15
and misogyny, 102
narratives of, 31,35
and Native Americans, 35
nature of, 5
New Age self-help, 30
and the 1950s, 36
and the 1992 Los Angeles race
    riots, 56
and the Olympics, 40
pervasiveness of, 37
political, 86-88,90
as political action, 4,103,105
political symbolism in, 86,87,90
as political tool, 86
as popular memory, 4,21,28,49,
    59,85
production of, 74-75,77-80
    and budgets, 70-71,72
    and facilities, 71-72
    and fluffers, 75-76
    and locations, 72
    and on-set problems
        with sex, 75-77
    and performers' doubles, 76
    and set conditions, 69-72
and public sex, 100
Queer, 89-90
and racial minorities, 54-55
with racial themes, 53,55-57
and racial title treatments, 54
and racism, 53-57,59
and relationships between older
    and younger men, 58-59
in relation to heterosexual
    pornography, 101-103
and Renaissance Europe, 35
rental of, 54
and the Roman empire, 35
sadomasochist, 16-18,53,58,
    60,65,67
    and Amnesty International, 62
    and bodypiercing, 62
    and bondage, 63-64
    and consensuality, 62

content of, 62,64
and fetishism, 64
and the fetishization
    of straight men, 65-66
and gender roles, 65
and humiliation, 64-67
and the "leather career," 67
mis-en-scene of, 62-63
and objectification, 66
as popular memory, 67
and realism, 62-63
and the second coming out, 67
and torture, 62
and safe sex, 27-32,78-80,
    83,86-87
and safe sex disclaimers, 80
and self-reflexivity, 46-48,50-51
and sexism, 53
and sex roles, 21
as sexual documentary, 79,81
and sites of sex, 21
and sizeism, 53
structure of, 18
themes of, 38,42,54
titles as racial disclaimers, 55
title treatment of, 89
transgenderist, 73*n.*
and underground film 15-19,90
and unsafe sex, 79
as validation, 21-22,51,85
and the Vietnam War, 36-37
viewing as safe sex, 30
and violence, 53-54,59
visibility of, 99
and the Wild West, 35
Pornography, hardcore
    advent of, 8,9,14
Porn Stars
    and AIDS, 79
    in drag, 73
    employment of, 72-73,75
    and feminization, 73
    "gay for pay," 24-25,26,27,
        28,50,65
    hierarchy of, 25,26,28

image marketing of, 73-74
and martyrdom, 79
performance of, 77
and prostitution, 81
and response to AIDS, 82-83
and response to anti-gay violence,
    82-83
wages of, 70-71,70n.
Porn theaters
and fantasy, 100
in Times Square (New York), 100
"Pornutopia," 47
invention of, 45
Powerful II, 50
Powers, Matt, 28
Preston, John, 82
Promiscuity, 31-32
Pronger, Brian, 40,41
and orthodox sexuality, 102-103
and paradoxical sexuality, 102
Prostitutes of New York (PONY), 48
Prostitution
in Los Angeles, 81-82
and safe sex, 82
wages, 81
Purusha, 61

Queer cinema, 90
Queer movement, 89-90
Queer Nation, 31,89
Queer: The Movie, 89

Rage, Christopher, 18,63,70,89
video content, 64
Ramsey, Matt, 25
Ramsey, Mike, 23
Raunchy Ricans, 54,55
Rebel Without a Cause, 36
"Reeducation of desire," 22,27
Report of the Commission
    on Pornography
    and Obscenity, 14
Revenge: More Than I Can Take, 45

Ridiculous Theatrical Company
    (New York), 15
Rise, The, 46
Rocco, Pat, 14,77
Roger, 71
Rogers, Byron, 70
Rollins, Mathieu, 93
Romeo and Juliet, 35,42
Roseland (New York), 82
Rowberry, 12-13,15,17,27,44,
    54,72,89
Royalle, Candida, 101

Sadomasochism, 59-62
and biochemistry, 60
and bodypiercing, 61
and catharsis, 61
and emotional pain, 61
and ego-transcendence, 61
and fistfucking, 61
and gender roles, 61
and the leather community, 60
and physical pain, 61-62
and the recodification of violence,
    61
and a shift in consciousness,
    60-61
and spiritual philosophies, 61
and violence, 62
Safe sex, 22,27-32,81
clubs, 43n.
literature, 82
packets, 82
Safe Sex: The Ultimate Erotic Guide,
    82
Sandow, Eugen, 6
Sarandon, Susan, 82
Scorpio, 35
Scorpio Rising, 9,17
Scott, Steve, 43-44
Screwing Screw Ups, 76,83
Self-defense videos, 82-83
Self-mortification, verbal, 55
Senate (U.S.), 14
Sequential action image studies, 7

Sex clubs, 46
Sex Garage, 16,17,19
Sex industry, 48
Sex, Lies, and Video Cassettes, 47,83
Sex Magic, 71
Sex Shooters II, 48-49,88
Sextool, 16,17,19
Sexuality, and procreation, 1
Sexual repression, 101
Shakespeare, William, 35
Siebenand, Paul, 77
Sighs, 45
Simmons, Joe, 86
Sizing Up, 40
Slater, J.D., 79-81
Slave Fights Back, The, 8
Slaves For Sale, 8
Slave Workshop-Hamburg, 63
Smith, Jack, 9,15
Social Movements, 4
Some Like It Hot, 14
Song of the Loon, 18,35
Sprinkle, Annie, 101
Stag films, 7
    content of, 7
    definition of, 7
    and drag, 7
    and heterosexual hegemony, 7
Staley, Peter, 86
Steel Garters, 73*n*.
Stefano, Joey, 25,30,47,50,51,70,
    71,74,90,96
Sterling, Matt, 24,25,73-74
Stiff Game, A, 7
Stoltenberg, John, 101-103
Stone, Jack, 64
Stonewall riots, 3,10,11,14
Stryker Force, 50
Stryker, Jeff, 29,30,49-51,71,72-73,
    74-75,82,83,87-88
Studio X, 56-57
Styles, Joseph, 43*n*.
Summers, Danny, 71
Sum Yung Mahn, 56-57
Sunset Boulevard, 64

Surge Studios, 80
Surprise of a Knight, 7
Swann, Glenn, 82
Swanson, Gloria, 64
Swiss AIDS Foundation, 80

Take Back the Night, 82-83
Taylor, Butch, 91
Taylor, Scott, 43,64
Telegraphiste, Le, 7
That Boy, 19
That Cold Day in the Park, 90
Time and space, social control of, 99
Townsend, Larry, 60-61
Trash, 11
Travis, John, 24,25,36,69,73-74,75,
    76
Turan, Kenneth, 16
Turbo Charge, 28,80
Turned On, 34,43-44
1230 Melrose Place, 56
Twice a Man, 10

Underground film, 10,15
    and homoeroticism, 9-12
    and the law, 9-10
Unfriendly Persuasion, 62
Unsafe sex, among teenagers, 81
Urban Aboriginals, 60
Urban Life, 43*n*.

Valentino, Rudolph, 47
Variety, 16
Vicinus, Martha, 33
Video technology, advent of, 15,24
Village Voice, The, 74
Violence, 60
    anti-gay, 82-83
von Gloeden, Wilhelm, 6-7

Wall, F., 70
Warhol, Andy, 9,10-11,13,15,25-26

and homosexuality, 10
and pornography, 10
Waters, John, 12
Waugh, Tom, 7,37,53,59,61
Weber, Bruce, 25-26
Weeks, Jeffrey, 41
Weider, Joe, 8
West, Jim, 54
Western Photography Guild, 8
Whicher, Jane, 97
Whitman, Don, 8,9
Whorezine, 48
Wild One, The, 36
Williams, Linda, 77-78
Wockner, Rex, 96

Women Against Pornography
(WAP), 48,78,101
Wood, Natalie, 36
Woodlawn, Holly, 12
Working Stiffs, 54,58
Wrangler, Jack, 71

Yeager, Ryan, 88
Young, David, 72,75,77
Young, Jared, 47

Zen, Michael, 18
Zeus Studios, 63
Zito, Stephen F., 16

*For Product Safety Concerns and Information please contact
our EU representative GPSR@taylorandfrancis.com Taylor & Francis
Verlag GmbH, Kaufingerstraße 24, 80331 München, Germany*

T - #0146 - 270225 - C0 - 212/152/8 - PB - 9781560238522 - Gloss Lamination